MIDNIGHT CLEAR
A NOVEL

Jerry B. Jenkins & Dallas Jenkins

MIDNIGHT CLEAR
A NOVEL

Tyndale House Publishers, Inc.
Carol Stream, Illinois

Visit Tyndale's exciting Web site at www.tyndale.com

TYNDALE and Tyndale's quill logo are registered trademarks of Tyndale House Publishers, Inc.

Midnight Clear

Designed by Mark Lane II

Scripture taken from the New King James Version®. Copyright © 1982 by Thomas Nelson, Inc. Used by permission. All rights reserved.

Library of Congress Cataloging-in-Publication Data

Jenkins, Jerry B.
   Midnight clear / Jerry B. Jenkins, Dallas Jenkins.
      p. cm.
   ISBN-13: 978-1-4143-1659-8 (sc : alk. paper)
   ISBN-10: 1-4143-1659-3 (sc : alk. paper)
   1. Christmas stories. I. Jenkins, Dallas. II. Title.
   PS3560.E485M53 2007
   813'.54—dc22   2007023358

Printed in the United States of America

13 12 11 10 09 08 07
7 6 5 4 3 2 1

DEDICATION

To Frank and Erika Muller, whose marriage has remained inspirational and strong despite personal tragedy.

ACKNOWLEDGMENTS

Thanks to . . .

Amanda Jenkins, always faithful, patient, and
supportive

Becky Nesbitt, my favorite person in publishing

Jeremy Taylor, a great editor to work with

Wes Halula, who helped shape this story

ONE

||||||||||||||||||||||||||||||||||||||||||||||||||||||||||||||||||||||||||||||||||||||||||||||||||||||||||||||||||||||||||||||

Lefty

Lefty Boyle's rusted '76 Caprice sat half a football field from the other cars in the factory parking lot, and he was in it—head back, eyes closed, mouth open, drooling.

A loud knock on the window interrupted the Hallmark portrait.

The car door opened from the outside. "You alive in there?"

The voice belonged to Kamal, the janitor who'd served as Lefty's alarm clock for the past three days.

Lefty stirred. "Yeah."

With that word came a stench of alcohol and morning breath that almost startled Lefty fully awake. Almost.

"You're fifteen minutes late. Dale's looking for you, and he's more ticked than usual."

1

Lefty tried to sink back into sleep. Nothing to think about. No reminders of, well, anything. Sleep was good.

Kamal nudged Lefty's shoulder. "You hear what I said?"

Lefty opened his eyes a sliver, but the morning light blinded him. He saw just enough to be reminded of where he was. He didn't remember exactly how he had gotten there, but fortunately, routine was his guide. As long as he got to his work-place parking lot at the end of each night, he would be where he needed to be the next morning.

"Yeah, I'm coming. And thanks for making me late!"

"Oh, gee, I'm sorry! My boss, who pays me, wanted me to do something more important than waking you up. Next time I'll tell him I work for Lefty."

For a foreigner, Kamal had an impressive grasp of American sarcasm.

Lefty grabbed his mangled toothbrush from the visor and stumbled out of the car. The effects of sleeping upright for six hours, combined with his usual morning headache, nearly caused him to col-lapse. He steadied himself against his car, rubbed his eyes, and took a deep, nasty breath. He found the factory entrance up ahead, trained his eyes, and headed toward it.

Two minutes later, his shoes shuffled across the

sticky floor of the factory bathroom. Lefty brushed his teeth and smoothed his greasy hair. He noticed a mustard stain on his shirt and, thinking quickly, turned the shirt inside out and took another glance at himself.

The shirt idea was a good one. Perhaps today had some promise. And wasn't it the twenty-fourth? Yeah, the last day before a holiday break for a few days. He could make it through today no problem. He straightened his shoulders and stared confidently at the image of himself before spotting his boss behind him in the grime-spotted mirror.

"Hey, Princess," Dale said, "when you're done putting on your makeup, get your royal behind into my office." The door slammed behind him.

Lefty's shoulders returned to their slumped position.

Merry Christmas.

Kirk

It wasn't even 8:30 in the morning, and Kirk was tired. Not a good sign.

The call had awakened him at 6:30. Kirk found it hard to believe that his seventeen-year-old employee had magically fallen sick the day before Christmas, but he was at least impressed the kid got up that early to call him. *If only he was as committed to his work . . .*

The fact that it was Christmas Eve wasn't what

annoyed Kirk about coming in. He had no special plans, and he wasn't a big holiday guy anyway. It was more that he had gotten his hopes up about sleeping in today. Kirk took only a handful of days off each year; and when he did, he slept in till noon, worked on the porch he'd been building for years, and relaxed. He'd been looking forward to today for over a week, and he'd been in the middle of some deep sleep when he was informed that this day would be the same as the 360 or so other mind-numbing days of the year.

Kirk wheeled into Mr. K's Quick Stop and parked in his usual spot, off to the side, amid loose gravel and tall weeds, close to the woods. He glanced up at the rusted sign. *Good grief, what a cheesy name.* That he was responsible for it made it worse.

He unlocked the door and two padlocks and stepped inside. His place. Four rows of "convenient" goods (healthy food was inconvenient, apparently) in front of a wall of beverages and frozen food. The side wall bore random fishing items and included a tiny, greasy eating area no longer open for business. Large banners, depicting beer and cigarettes consumed by people who looked nothing like his customers, hung from the ceiling.

For most gas stations of this ilk, opening meant turning on the pumps, the cash register, and the food machines. But try as he might, Kirk couldn't break the routine he'd started when he first bought the place and actually gave a rip. Toilet scrubbed. Garbage emptied. Soap dispenser filled. Paper towel and napkin canisters loaded. Merchandise organized. And, of course, brewing the gourmet coffee. He knew that offering gourmet coffee at a place like this was akin to offering a filet mignon at a hot dog stand. His store and his customers didn't deserve gourmet coffee. But he couldn't do the instant stuff. Just couldn't.

He finished the brew, wiped down the counters, and tossed some loose trash. For the local trailer park families, shirtless smokers, meth addicts, fishermen, and long-distance travelers who thought the Southwest would be a good Christmas location, Mr. K's Quick Stop was ready.

Sorry, We're Closed became *Yes, We're Open!*
Merry Christmas.

Eva

Eva was determined that her death would cause no complications for anyone, and since today was the day—or rather, tonight would be the night—she thought it best to prepare.

She trudged through her house toward the kitchen, running through a mental checklist of the tasks she needed to accomplish today. She had always made a point of ensuring nothing was left undone or turned on when she left the house for vacation; she certainly wanted to make sure of the same now that she was leaving her house forever.

As Eva grabbed the cat food bag from her kitchen counter for the last time, it wasn't sadness or remorse she felt. Just a sense of duty. She would accomplish her tasks today with calm and dignity. She would not cry, she would not be overly sentimental, and she would not act scared. This would be like any other day, just perhaps a little busier.

Eva lugged the bag out to her driveway and, leaning against the house, bent and filled the bowl. The sound brought Scrappy, the neighborhood stray, running. As the cat dug in, Eva emptied the rest of the food onto the concrete. Scrappy would need enough to last however long it took for someone to discover Eva's body.

Merry Christmas.

Mary

Mary pulled into the drop-off spot at the elementary school a bit too fast. Her morning routine with Jacob always seemed rushed now that she was raising him on her own. At six years old, Jacob had no problem getting up at 6:45 every morning. But Mary did. She would turn on the Disney Channel for him, go back to bed for half an hour, then slam through the morning to get him to school by 8:15 and herself to work by 8:30. It helped that she didn't need to look flawless and that she and Jacob were both fine with

Nutri-Grain bars in the minivan as their breakfast of champions.

Jacob's too-cute teacher, wearing a too-cute Santa hat, bounced out to greet them. "Hey, Jacob!" Megan said. "How're you doing, buddy?"

Jacob smiled and waved, unbuckling his seat belt.

Megan's smile vanished, and she cocked her head. *Here it comes.*

"Hey, Mary. You doing okay?"

"I'm fine. You?"

"Seriously. You doing all right?" Megan lowered her voice, as if to emphasize the seriousness of her question.

Mary paused. Megan wasn't going to let her off the hook, especially today. "As well as can be expected. Seriously."

Thankfully, Jacob struggled with the door, and Megan rushed to help him out of the van.

As he ran off, Mary called out, "Love you, Jacob! Be good!"

Without turning or slowing, he hollered, "Love you!"

Mary turned back to Megan. "His juice box is in his backpack. He'll try to tell you I forgot to give him—"

"Got it." Megan smiled knowingly, then looked puzzled, peering in at Mary. "Hey, you know those seats *are* adjustable."

Mary had been riding low in the seat, reaching for the wheel, for a year and had gotten used to it.

"Oh. Yeah. Well, this is the way Rick liked it, though. I just . . . you know . . ."

Megan backed off. "Yeah. Okay. See you at noon?"

Finally.

"See you at noon."

Today was December 24. This conversation would not be the last of its kind, Mary was sure. *People are just trying to be nice,* she reminded herself.

Merry Christmas.

Mitch

Mitch exchanged his car for the fifteen-passenger van in the church parking lot. The van needed gas for a dozen small trips all afternoon and evening. This jaunt to the gas station would mark the only time he would be in it without a load of loud teenagers.

It was going to be a miserable day, plain and simple. In six hours, when he had to take his youth group kids caroling, it would get really miserable. But this was also the one-year anniversary of the accident.

A year before, Mitch's car had been in the shop, so Rick, his best friend and one of the youth leaders, gave him a ride home from the church youth party. The drunk driver never slowed as he raced through the intersection and rammed the driver's side of Rick's car. Mitch suffered cracked ribs and a separated shoulder when Rick's body drove him into the passenger door.

Mitch had needed a sling and bandages. Rick had needed epic, emergency surgery. A year later, he was still institutionalized.

Everything had changed that night. *Everything.* Rick wasn't really Rick anymore. On the rare days he was settled enough to have a moderately coherent conversation, they had nothing to talk about. Most days Rick was like a two-year-old, everything included—tantrums, diapers, you name it. Either way, the casualness and shared sense of humor that had defined their friendship were gone, replaced by awkward small talk.

Mitch hadn't visited him in weeks; it was too hard, and the visits didn't seem to do much for Rick anyway.

Now, as Mitch passed through the same intersection, he got that same chill and couldn't keep from looking both ways repeatedly. He'd passed through it hundreds of times in the past year, but it was always the same. Every time, random details of the accident flashed in his mind. The screaming of a woman bystander, the blood pooling in Mitch's lap, the flashing lights of half a dozen cop cars and ambulances. Every time, he shuddered and felt weak because of his reaction.

The fact that the accident had taken place on Christmas Eve made forgetting or ignoring the

one-year anniversary impossible, even if he had
wanted to. Eventually, Christmas Eves might feel
normal again. But so far, this one wasn't looking
good.

Merry Christmas.

||||||||||||||||||||||||||||||||||||||||||||||||||||||||||||||||||||||||||||||||||||||||||||||||||||||||||||||||||||||||||||||||||||||||||||||||||

Lefty

Dale was a good guy to work for. Sure, he talked
tough, rarely smiled, and obviously cared deeply
about running a great cement plant. But he couldn't
help treating his workers right, try as he might to act
tough. If someone screwed up, Dale made sure he
knew it—along with everyone within earshot—and
said offender never did it again. But word was, Dale
supported his people to the brass without exception,
and everyone knew the harsh side of him was overwhelmed by the side that would step in front of a bus
for his men.

Lefty was praying to see that step-in-front-of-a-
bus side of Dale today.

History wasn't in his favor. No one saw the harsh
Dale more than the Assistant Production Line Supervisor of Chuck & Mike's Cement. But by now, getting

yelled at had become part of Lefty's life, so he was prepared for the verbal spanking he'd get for being late yet again. Lefty knew that Dale was angry mostly because when Lefty wasn't there, neither were his obvious mechanical skills. It was flattering.

Lefty knew he wasn't cut out for white-collar work. He wasn't exactly the suit-and-tie type. But he had done pretty well in shop class in high school, so when he quit his pizza-place job after graduation, he'd figured he could succeed at hands-on jobs. He'd had several in the last decade, but none of them was "quite the right fit." The factory gig had come along thanks to a worker whom Lefty had met at the race-track. An old man had just died, they were looking for someone, and Lefty had loaned the guy five bucks for a bet, so the guy had gotten him an interview with Dale.

Lefty had been working at the factory for a year and a half now, and he knew that this was the kind of place where his skills were appreciated. His recent promotion had confirmed that, and Lefty figured Dale was hard on him only because he knew Lefty had so much potential.

Now, as he stepped into Dale's office, Lefty tried to get in a few words before Dale's inevitable erup-tion.

"Say, Dale, I'm gonna need an extended lunch break today. I've got this meeting with my wife's law-yers, and—"

"You must be joking."

Lefty sat. "No, Dale, I'm not. Now I know what you're think—"

"What is wrong with you, Lefty? Am I nuts, or did we have a conversation yesterday? What else can I do for you? I got you that promotion. Nobody thought it was a good idea, but I pushed it. And you thank me by being late every day since. *Every day!* How is that possible?"

Lefty smirked. "It's pretty easy, actually."

"Oh, you think this is funny. I can't believe I wasted my time on you."

"Look, Dale, I appreciate the promotion; I do. But you've gotta understand, now that I'm making more money, I admit I've been partyin' a little bit more. But I guarantee it will not affect my work." Lefty tapped the table for emphasis.

Dale stared at him. "Please tell me you're not that stupid. I gave you a promotion. You didn't get a raise. *Assistant Production Line Supervisor?* It doesn't mean anything; it's just a name." Dale leaned forward, quieting. "I did it for your custody case because I knew it'd look good for the judge and your kids. But you take that charity and you blow it up in my face. I'm not blind; I know you're drinking again."

Lefty couldn't argue with that one. He had promised Dale a year ago that he would drink only on weekends, but that had lasted about a week. His next binge sent him back to Alcoholics Anonymous.

They always loved to see him coming; he was a classic. He could stay sober for weeks, but when he disappeared, he might not turn up again for a year. Lately, he thought he'd done a good job of hiding it, but someone must have ratted him out.

"You're hopeless, Lefty. Stinks to hear it, I know, but somebody's gotta tell you. I'm sorry, man; I gotta do it."

"Now hold on a minute, Dale. This place would shut down without me. Who else is gonna change all those belts on the line?"

"Anyone with opposable thumbs. Playtime's over. Clear out your locker and go home. You're fired. An escort will take you to your car." Dale turned back to his computer.

This was not the first time Lefty had heard those words. But this was particularly bad timing. How would he spin this to his ex-wife? to the judge? He had no contingency plan.

"Now, Dale—"

"Go home, Lefty."

Eva

In all the movies or TV shows Eva watched where someone was suicidal, a monumental event always jump-started the process, some consequence the character couldn't bear. "I can't live without Julia!" or "I'm not going back to jail, man!"

Suicide notes had common threads as well. Long

and detailed or short and simple, the notes had a heavy amount of self-loathing and fear. Eva remembered hearing on the news that Kurt Cobain's "I hate myself and I want to die" had been put on a poster with his picture and had sold well.

Eva didn't hate herself. Not that she was a huge fan, but she thought she was okay. She had to look at herself in the mirror every morning and night, and she didn't mind it. And while she'd made her share of mistakes in life, there were no significant consequences coming up that she dreaded. Those already existed—estrangement from family, barely surviving on Social Security, painful memories, yada yada yada. She'd gotten used to all that.

Here was the thing:

She simply had no reason to live.

Was that so difficult to understand? She'd lived a long life, and it hadn't worked out all that well. Plain and simple. She didn't need sympathy, and she wasn't desperate for new friends. Fact was, nothing around the bend would make her life better or worse than it was now. Yes, even something worse would be better than this. If something were coming that would make her life worse, she might stick around for it. At least it would be interesting.

And wasn't that the point? To walk through life waiting for something interesting? Or to at least be interesting to others, like celebrities were? Happy people with close friends or family had additional benefits, of course. But Eva didn't have close friends or family, and she hadn't for a while. And she had no energy to create anything interesting, no skills to make someone else's life interesting.

She was old and tired. More important, she was unnecessary. These may not be reasons you'd see in a suicide story featured on *ER*, but they were good enough for her.

Mary

There was a time when Mary would have thought that someone raising a child alone would crave company, that the drive to work would be even lonelier than time at home. But now, her drive to work was her only time to herself without responsibilities.

Exhausted didn't even begin to describe Mary.

When she was a stay-at-home mom, that had been exhausting. But she'd had the promise of Rick's return at the end of the day. Chores, worry, discipline, Jacob's playtime—they were all shared. Because the frustrations of raising a child were softened by having a partner to help deal with them, she had been able to appreciate the joys that much more. She loved being a full-time mother, and even when the days were long, there was still adult conversation, cuddling, or sex to look forward to.

No longer.

Mary adored Jacob. She not only loved him, but she also genuinely liked him. Not all parents can say that about their kids. He was smart and gentle, not unlike his father. And at the end of her workday, she drove way too fast to go pick him up from school because she ached to see him. Twice during the last year she'd been caught speeding on her way to pick him up.

But Mary's life was consumed with responsibility and effort, and Jacob represented the biggest chunk of that. While driving to work, she knew he was taken care of and would be for the next seven hours. She could relax.

Whenever Mary had driven by herself before December 24 of last year, she'd used the first few minutes to pray. She was a big fan of talk radio, and her instinct was to turn it on the moment she started the car. But she resolved that her reach for the dial would be her reminder to pray, and she'd held to it. Of course, during particularly tumultuous political times, her prayers were short. Overall, though, she did well.

But after Rick's accident, she had quit praying. Well, that wasn't entirely true. At first she had been obsessed with prayer. She didn't need the radio dial to remind her to pray. She prayed nearly every waking moment.

Please don't let Rick suffer.
Please show me how to take care of Jacob.
Please don't let him grow up without a dad.
Please keep me strong.

Please let me accept Your will.

Please heal Rick.

Please let him live a normal life.

The Bible says to pray without ceasing, and for two weeks after the accident, she had. It hadn't worked.

Mary didn't have any interest in talk radio anymore, so the car stayed silent. And Mary was no longer a praying woman.

Mitch

Normally the intern would handle mundane tasks like filling the church van with gas. But Mitch wanted to get away today. He didn't want the questions or concerned looks about what this day meant. Of course, getting out and driving alone meant he had no distractions and was left to dwell on not-so-fond memories, so he couldn't win either way. He just had to accept that today was going to be a rough reminder of what happened a year ago.

Fine, he could plow through it. Other people dealt with worse. Like Rick.

Because the van needed a lot of gas, Mitch headed for a cheap station on the outskirts of town. It was tucked behind a popular fishing lake near a forested community of trailers where mangy dogs were as common as shoes were rare.

This neighborhood would not be a target for caroling tonight.

Sheesh, the caroling.

Mitch had been assigned the joyous task of taking his youth group to sing to some of the church members who didn't get out much or were likely to need cheering up. Translation: old people.

Mitch had been the youth pastor at Grace Fellowship for almost two years. At twenty-seven, he was relatively young to be in charge of the high schoolers in a church of four thousand members. He had graduated from Dallas Theological Seminary and was a sought-after youth leader. Grace was a well-known church pastored by Mark Russell, whose books and radio sermons had inspired Mitch. Being associate youth pastor here had been a great opportunity, even if the money wasn't great.

Two years into Mitch's tenure, the youth pastor had retired, and Mitch had been promoted. This was what he'd wanted to do since high school. Not only was it a stable job doing something he enjoyed, but he believed in it. He would impact these kids forever, be one of their most important influencers during the most volatile time of their lives. He would teach them about their faith, and some would find God for the first time.

To dispel the notion that church was boring or stodgy, Mitch made Sunday mornings and Wednesday nights a blast. Rick, one of the volunteer leaders who'd been there for almost a decade, had advised Mitch and helped him develop the Grace Fellowship high school program into one of the most dynamic youth groups in the area.

But then came the accident. The momentum was shot.

Now, as Mitch pulled into the run-down gas station in the middle of White Trash County, gassing up so he could drive a group of teenagers to sing "Joy to the World" to shut-ins, he wasn't sure he wanted to be a youth pastor anymore.

Kirk

Kirk stood behind the counter. Better said, he leaned against the cigarette wall behind the counter. This was what he would do the rest of the day. Because of the holiday, there would be no deliveries from vendors, and because he had no help, he would have to handle all the customers.

He remembered caring whether the day was busy. He'd been happy to be overworked and overwhelmed with customers. Busy meant profitable. Profitable meant attractive to potential area real estate buyers.

Now it didn't matter. He was stuck with this station for the rest of his life. By the time he might be able to pay it off and get in the black, he would be too old to benefit from it, and he had no family to pass the benefits along to anyway.

Daily sales hadn't fluctuated more than a hundred dollars in the eight years Kirk had owned the place. Sure, gas prices made a difference in raw numbers, but not in profit. Mr. K's made most of its money from the convenience items anyway, particularly cigarettes and lotto tickets. He didn't offer premium gasoline because his customers didn't care. People came to Mr. K's for cheap fuel and their vices.

The annoying door chime signaled the first customer.

The guy shuffled in and tossed a wrinkled twenty on the counter. "Pump one."

He shuffled out.

The morning crowd was always the quickest and quietest. These weren't the locals. The locals weren't up this early. These were fishing tourists or laborers on their way to blue-collar jobs. Gas, maybe coffee and cigarettes, was all they wanted. Most were uninterested in chitchat or even eye contact. That was fine with Kirk.

Kirk turned the pump one key and settled back into his spot before noticing a box of canned cranberries he'd forgotten to shelve sitting under the counter. He'd special-ordered them for Christmas—no big deal, just something different. He began setting the cans next to the register.

THREE
9:00 A.M.

||||||||||||||||||||||||||||||||||||||||||||||||||||||||||||||||||||||||||||||||||||||||||||||||||||||||||||||||||||

Mitch

Mitch squeezed the nozzle handle. Nothing. Was it possible this place was out of gas? He honked his horn, then waved toward the store.

The weary attendant opened the door. "Prepay only, Christmas Eve or any other day!"

"Ah, I guess that would explain the sign right in front of my eyes that says 'Prepay Only,' huh?"

At least that made the guy chuckle.

Prepay only, even during the day. Ha. Said a lot about the local clientele.

This kind of place always confused Mitch. He noticed the rusted sign, the massive chunk taken out of the overhang above the pumps. Did the owner simply not care about the place anymore? That seemed to be the attitude of everyone in this neighborhood. The shortest lawn was at least five inches, and as if out of a Jeff Foxworthy joke book, every driveway contained an out-of-commission car. The people who lived in these homes did not represent the constituency of Mitch's church; that was for sure.

Kirk

Kirk was convinced that most people who had to be reminded that his pumps were prepay hadn't intended to pay in the first place. Many just drove off after their foiled attempts, some of them repeat customers.

This customer looked fine. Young, decent-looking guy. Clean-cut, all-American type. Represented about 3 percent of Kirk's patrons. Probably a tourist. Kirk finished stacking his cranberry cans on the counter while the guy walked toward the coffeepot.

"Kinda lousy working on Christmas Eve, huh?"

Kirk looked up. "Huh?"

"Christmas Eve? Not fun?"

"Oh . . . uh, yeah. I guess." Did this guy really want a conversation?

"Boss gave you the raw deal, huh?"

He *did* want conversation.

"You're looking at him."

"Oh yeah?" the guy said. "Then why the heck are you working today?"

Kirk hadn't heard *heck* in years.

"Kid didn't show up to work today, called in sick. What else am I gonna do?"

"Kids aren't the most dependable creatures." He put the coffee down on the counter. "This, plus fifty bucks on two. So do you even have to be open today?"

"Chug-a-lug and Neighbor Mart are closed. I'd be stupid to pass up the Christmas Eve rush."

The guy turned to survey the store, kind enough not to mention that they were the only two there. "Uh, yeah."

"Fifty-one oh five."

"Thanks; keep the change. Merry Christmas."

The guy turned to leave. He took a sip of coffee, then did a double take.

Kirk looked up. "Problem?"

"No, it's really good, actually."

Definitely not a regular. Regular customers didn't give that look of surprise anymore. They knew how good the coffee was. Kirk had to admit he missed that look.

When Kirk first opened Mr. K's, he'd intended it to be a uniquely customer-friendly gas station. As this guy walked out, Kirk realized he had just had his longest conversation with a customer in five years.

Lefty

Kamal walked Lefty to his car.

"Where's Security?" Lefty said. "You'd think they'd at least have Security take me out."

"Security's got sensitivity training today."

"Yeah, well, this isn't very sensitive."

They arrived at the car. Kamal put his hand on Lefty's shoulder. "Go home, Lefty."

"Well, that's gonna be kinda hard, seeing as how you're standing in the middle of my living room."

Kamal chuckled and, surprising Lefty, gave him a hug. "Good luck, buddy."

Lefty nodded and slid behind the wheel. When he turned the key, the fuel gauge was buried close to *E*.

"Hey, Kamal! You got a fiver? Just till payday?"

Kamal kept walking.

As Lefty threw the old beater into drive, he got an idea. There weren't too many ways he could exact revenge on Dale for the firing. But he could make a statement by stealing something from the factory before he went on his way. Of course, he wasn't sure what point it would make, and he didn't want Dale to know it was him making the statement. But it would be a statement.

Because Security was in training, no doubt learning how to better deal with thieves, Lefty didn't worry too much about getting caught. He simply pulled up next to one of the storage sheds, grabbed four tubs of paint, and tossed them into his trunk. He peeled out of the factory with a smirk.

This was the kind of thing that gave him a rush, a feeling he didn't get too often. Was it guilt? Nah. Losing this paint wouldn't cripple the company. But the fact was, at some point soon someone would need the paint, and it would be missing. Someone would need something Lefty had. And even on a small scale, that was rare. It significantly outweighed any guilt or fear of getting caught.

Eva

As she waited on hold with the clinic, Eva emptied her fridge and freezer into a garbage bag. She didn't want anyone to have to clear trash or worry about spoiled items.

"—inic, can I help you?"

"Yes," Eva said, "I had an appointment with Dr. Lindell yesterday, and I was a little confused about some of the medications he'd given me. I—"

"Hold plea—" *Click.* Music.

"Yes, I can hold."

Eva tossed the ketchup into the bag.

"Dr. Lindell."

"Hello, hi, this is Eva Boyle. I had an appointment with Dr. Lindell last week and—"

"This *is* Dr. Lindell. Hi, Eva."

"Oh, Dr. Lindell, I wasn't expecting you!"

"Our appointment was yesterday."

"Oh yes, it was yesterday. I knew that; I said that to the other lady. I swear, if you could give me something for this head of mine—"

"How can I help you, Eva?"

"Well, I know I'm supposed to take some of my medicines in the morning, and some—"

"Yes, you copied my instructions, remember? Do you still have that paper?"

"Oh, I did, didn't I? Oh, you're right. I have it right here on the counter next to my fridge! I feel so silly."

Eva held up two bottles of pills, one with a red label and one with a yellow.

"That's fine, Eva. Just remember to match the colors."

"Right, red with red and yellow with yellow. Thank you so much. I'm sorry I wasted your time. I just remembered you telling me that I need to be careful which ones I took with which and when."

"All right, Eva. Merry Christmas."

"Thank you, and merry Christmas to you, too, Dr. Lindell."

Eva hung up the phone. She was sure Dr. Lindell didn't suspect anything. In fact, at her appointment the day before, she'd told him about her big family dinner coming up on Christmas. ". . . coming in from all over, first time in two years."

She didn't want anyone to worry, and she didn't want any visits or phone calls today. She figured she deserved that much on her last day.

Mary

Mary knew nothing about the software her company manufactured, but she was good at her job. Two months after Rick's accident, she'd gotten a job as

Office Assistant at Global Scope Software, which meant she ran around making sure the owner and eight employees had what they needed. Within a month, she had the office so organized and running so efficiently that they created the Office Manager position for her.

Everyone reported to the boss for employment-related issues, but everything else was Mary's territory. Nothing was filed, transferred, reimbursed, delivered, accepted, or organized without her sign-off. She wasn't anyone's boss, but the real boss didn't want to deal with this stuff, so Mary took care of it all.

She'd made it clear from the beginning that she wouldn't work past the end of Jacob's school day. Seven hours a day, not a minute more. She proved so good and efficient that her boss had no problem with her hours.

Trudy, the fiftyish office mom and customer service rep, poked her head over Mary's cubicle wall. "I can't believe we're working right now."

Once, a couple months earlier, a drunk flirt had refused to leave Mary alone at a sports bar during their lunch break, and Trudy had punched him in the nose. This was the woman who brought homemade banana bread to work every Friday and had pictures of six grandchildren on her desk next to her Bible. Mary loved her.

"Thanks for reminding me," Mary said, sighing.

"I actually think we're hurting our customers here."

"Oh, come on."

"No, I worked out this theory. See, if you need tech support on Christmas Eve, then that means you have no life. And if you have no life, shouldn't we do our part to help you get a life by being closed so that you're forced to go out and actually see people face-to-face for a change?"

"Yeah, well . . . I'm not sure I'd go that far, but it's a nice theory."

"Isn't it, though?"

Mary kept typing. "I'm just trying to make the best of it, maybe get ahead on some reports."

"Going for early retirement?"

"Not that far ahead."

"Let me know when you're closing in on it—oh no! I'm getting a call. Should I answer it?"

"Yes!"

"But my theory—"

"Answer it!"

Trudy clicked her headset. "Global Scope Software, this is Trudy; may I have your account number please?" She paused for effect but didn't move. "Okay, what seems to be the trouble? Hmm, oh my. Let me look up your service record." Another fake pause as she rolled her eyes at Mary. "Open—uh-oh—our server has just shut down. Isn't that annoying? I do apologize. Maybe you should go spend Christmas Eve with your family."

Mary stifled a laugh.

"Right, call back on Monday. Okay then. Have I answered all of your questions? I know technically I haven't; I'm just supposed to ask you that. Okay, talk to you on Monday. 'Bye."

"Trudy, you're going to get yourself fired."

"Yeah, maybe, but I don't want to be here today anyway! We're supposed to be with our families today. I mean, come on!"

Mary busied herself to hide the awkwardness.

"I'm sorry," Trudy said suddenly.

"Don't be. You should be with your family."

"Are you, um . . . going to see Rick today?"

"Yeah, for a little bit. Then Jacob and I are going to my folks' house."

"That's good. Mary, I'm so sorry. I didn't mean—"

"Stop it. I'm fine. Honestly, I'm glad we're working today. I think I'd lose it if I didn't have something to do."

"Then I'm glad I'm here with you too. So are you taking Jacob to see Rick?"

Mary smiled, nodded.

"Well, that's good; that's good. Oh, you are kidding me! I'm getting another call. What is wrong with these people!" Obviously grateful for the distraction, Trudy returned to her cubicle.

The one-year anniversary of the accident. Everyone knew it, and their efforts to put on happy faces were as unending as they were frustrating. Why is it that when someone suffers a tragedy they have to work so hard to keep everyone else from feeling awkward?

FOUR

11:00 A.M.

||||||||||||||||||||||||||||||||||||||||||||||||||||||||||||||||||||||||||||||||||||||||||||||||||||||||||||||||||

Mitch

So far Mitch hadn't had to deal with any awkward conversations. Of course, it wasn't as if he were on everyone's mind today, even if they remembered the accident. He was physically fine now, so any sympathy was rightly directed toward Rick, Rick's wife, Mary, and their son, Jacob.

Regardless, everyone at church was preoccupied with the big Christmas Eve service, so no one talked to Mitch anyway.

Mary hadn't been back to church since the accident. She never expressed outright anger to anyone, and she'd told Mitch right away that she didn't blame him for what happened. She just wouldn't feel comfortable there, and Mitch couldn't blame her. Who would want that much attention, especially over something so personal and devastating?

33

Mitch made copies of the Christmas carols for tonight. He chuckled at the musical notes on the pages—as if the kids could read music. They weren't going to sound too good anyway, but if they didn't already know these songs, musical notation wasn't going to help.

Pastor Mark walked in, carrying a festive basket trimmed with Christmas ribbons and filled with a stack of thick envelopes. "Hey, Mitch. I put these packets together for you to give out tonight. There's a card, a Christmas CD, and twenty bucks in each one."

Mitch looked at the basket. Each envelope was labeled with the name of a recipient, and Mitch knew Mark well enough to know that each contained a unique, handwritten note. The touch was nothing if not personal.

"Twenty bucks? Isn't that kind of insulting?"

"I don't think so. I'd rather give out something people might actually need than some tree ornament or a candy cane. They can always use money—for food, bus fare, whatever."

"Yeah, well, I'm just not sure how they're gonna take it."

Mark helped sort the pages for each kid's caroling folder. Of course he did. He never stopped helping.

"I gather you're not too excited about tonight?"

"Not tremendously, no. We're talking high school students here. The last thing they wanna do is go

caroling for old people. I mean, it's not 1948 anymore."

"Fair enough, Mitch, but frankly, I'm not too concerned with what they, or you, want to do. Not every
act of service is a joyride." He stopped and cocked his
head. "Is some of this about what day it is? I know it
was a year ago tonight."

Mitch wanted to be annoyed that Mark had
brought it up. He also wanted to play dumb and say
that his frustration was solely about the caroling.
But . . .

"Maybe, I guess."

"This could be good for you, actually. Get your
mind off it, focus on others, do something nice . . ."

"Or cheesy."

"Most of the people you're visiting tonight are
shut-ins. You'll be the only people they see over the
holidays. Others haven't been to church for a while
and aren't sure if anyone here still cares about them.
Might mean a lot to bring a little church to them."

"Yeah, we've been through this."

"Let me put it another way. Not everything you do
with the kids has to be cool or hip. It's good for them
to just do some ministry once in a while."

"But you know kids are fickle. These kids haven't
all decided if I'm worth listening to anyway, and this
is the kind of thing that could push them over the
line. And once they're on the other side, you can just
bury me and hire a new seminary grad."

The fact was, the idea of a new seminary grad taking over for Mitch wasn't altogether horrifying to him. What a weird thought. From the time Mitch graduated from high school, he couldn't imagine doing anything but this, and everything had gone according to plan. What was wrong with him?

"Well, at least you're overly dramatic. I'm sure they can identify with that."

Mitch knew he deserved that. He was whining. He was annoying himself. It had been that kind of day. That kind of year, for that matter.

"You want them to decide if you're worth listening to?" Mark said. "*Be* worth listening to. Get passionate about this stuff. Show them a faith that's strong enough to make them want to do things they wouldn't normally do." He turned to leave. "I gotta go. I'll see you at the service later."

Mitch couldn't argue with Mark, of course. The whole point of being a youth pastor was to inspire kids to be more passionate about their faith and to do something meaningful with their lives. He would love to show them a faith strong enough to make them want to do things they wouldn't normally do. He would love to *have* that faith.

Mark stopped at the door. "And, Mitch . . . technically, old people are still people."

"I don't think that's true, but I'll look it up on the Internet later."

Mark smiled. "Do that."

And he was gone.

Mitch decided then and there that tonight would be something of a litmus test. If he could find some relevance, passion, or significance from tonight's outing, in the midst of all that this night represented, he would jump-start his ministry. But if he couldn't get past all his issues, legitimate or not, and if tonight didn't revive any of his passion, he would consider another career. He was tired of pouting.

Lefty

Lefty hadn't changed his clothes in three days. Showering had meant wiping himself down with wet paper towels in the factory bathroom. His schedule for the past week had consisted of work, hanging out at Frank's Pub, a visit or two to the casino, and sleeping—in his car, of course.

As he pulled into the parking lot of the Lester, Meyer, and Bernson law firm building, he knew that his frayed, white (turning yellow) thermal shirt and work jacket wouldn't suffice in a professional setting. He fished around in the backseat and found a red sweater. It was on the loud side, but maybe it would seem Christmassy. Plus, wasn't a sweater the equivalent of a shirt and tie? He took off his jacket and pulled the sweater over his thermal. His hair was greasy enough that it didn't get too messed up in the exchange.

Fourteen minutes later, Lefty sat alone in a huge

conference room, nursing a glass of water. If the goal of the opulent room was to make visitors and opponents feel out of their league, it worked. His ex-wife's parents had helped pay for her big-time lawyers. Heather's folks had never been happy with the marriage (eloping hadn't helped) and were more than willing to speed up the divorce process and make sure their daughter got every edge.

Finally, two men and a woman in tailored suits bustled in.

"You're Luschel, right?" The middle-aged man hurried toward Lefty and handed him a business card.

Lefty started to stand.

"Don't get up. I'm Gordon Lester. I'll be working with Samantha Lewis, representing your ex-wife from here on out. I know you two have met. And this is Greg, our file clerk."

Samantha, on her cell phone, nodded at Lefty.

Greg laid out all their materials on the conference table. No one made eye contact.

Lefty took a sip. "Lefty."

Gordon looked up. "Excuse me?"

"Everyone calls me Lefty."

Samantha rolled her eyes and covered the receiver. "His nickname. Cute as it is, Luschel, we won't be using that today. I'm sure you understand." She whispered something into the phone and snapped it shut.

Greg pressed a button on a digital recorder on the table and mouthed, "We are recording," circling his finger to illustrate.

"It's just that everyone calls me Lefty." Lefty leaned in toward the mic. "Lefty. For the record."

"Of course they—"

"I'm a lefty too," Gordon interrupted Samantha. "Born that way."

Silence.

Lefty continued, "It's weird, though, on account I'm not even left-handed."

Gordon looked around. "Where's your representation?"

"Um, I . . . my lawyer and I don't see eye to eye on things anymore. Anyway, everyone's called me Lefty since I was a kid because we were pretty poor, and—"

"You don't have a lawyer?"

"Right. So, since we didn't have much money, if I wanted to play ball, I had to use my brother's left-handed baseball glove. So I wasn't any good because of that. But the other kids didn't know that I was right-handed. They just thought that . . . well, they just thought that I wasn't any good."

Samantha smirked. "All righty. Greg, we need mochas."

The file clerk hustled out.

Gordon leaned in and looked intently at Lefty. "Sir, you realize that you have the right to have legal representation with you? And since you've chosen not to have counsel present, you waive all rights to such protection as would be provided by state statutes regarding said representation?"

Lefty stared at him.

Samantha spoke slowly. "You're okay with not having a lawyer here?"

"Right."

"Good," she said. "I'll speak my mind, then. I advised the court against this. I think you're a terrible father, and—"

"I think what Ms. Lewis is getting at," Gordon said, "is that this agreement is tenuous at best. We know it, your ex-wife knows it, and it's important that you know it too. So I would strongly suggest that you do everything in your power to retain your newly acquired visitation privileges. You realize this will require some, um, lifestyle changes?"

"I just got a promotion. I'll be getting a much nicer place real soon."

"Maybe we should just fill out this paperwork and be done. We just need to verify a few things and get some signatures. Are you still at 4742 Alcott Avenue?"

"Um—" Lefty leaned into the mic—"no."

"What's your current address?"

"Well, it's kind of complicated. See, I've got this landlord. He's, like, a real Nazi landlord. And he wouldn't let me slide for a few weeks, so—"

Lefty looked up. They were staring at him.

Apparently following Samantha's example, Gordon spoke slowly. "Are you telling us that you don't have a home or an apartment or any sort of shelter?"

"No, I have shelter. I just don't have an address at the moment."

Samantha chuckled. "What, are you living in your car?"

Lefty just stared at her, unable to think of a better way to put it.

Samantha looked to the ceiling. "You've got to be kidding."

Gordon gathered his paperwork. "Luschel, no court in the world is going to grant visitation rights to someone who is . . . homeless. We can't go through with this today." They stood to leave.

"No, you have to. The court said I'd have visitation; now that's a done deal."

Samantha turned to yell for Greg just as the clerk walked in and set down the mochas. She spoke quickly. "Call Sobel's courtroom and get a new hearing. Whatever it takes."

Greg hustled off again, and Gordon and Samantha turned to follow him.

"Please." Somehow the desperation in Lefty's voice stopped the lawyers, and they turned to face him. "My kids should see me. I'm gonna get a new place as soon as I get a new job. I—"

Samantha stepped forward. "A new job?"

"You said you just got a raise," Gordon said, wincing.

Lefty sighed. "It's complicated. I did get a promotion, but . . . I got fired right after that."

"I'm sorry, but we're required to report the information you've just given us to the court. We'll contact you when a new hearing is set up."

"But I can see my kids until then?"

"I'm afraid that can't happen. I'm sorry. Try to have a good day."

And they were gone.

Lefty had never been a good father. He knew that. He was never abusive, at least not physically. His drinking had never made him violent, just sullen and distant. But with parenting, he simply had no idea what he was doing. Even now, if he could get the one-weekend-a-month visits the court had awarded him, he wasn't sure what he would do with the kids.

But it was something he was desperate to work on. What else did he have? He hadn't done well as a full-time father, but he was sure he could handle a few days a month. Jordan and Katie actually liked him. When he wasn't drinking, he could be fun, and he wasn't going to drink around the kids ever again. Maybe he wasn't the wisest, most structured father in the world, but at least he wasn't his own dad, an abusive waste who unfortunately hadn't died until Lefty was an adult.

And now it didn't matter. These elitist jerks were

going to take away his chance to correct a few things in his life.

He stood and turned off the digital recorder. The lawyers had left a small stack of folders that looked important lying on the table. He stared at the folders, then shoved them onto the floor, scattering the papers. It wasn't revenge on an epic scale, but it was something.

As Lefty collected himself, Greg, the snot-nosed file clerk, returned. He saw the papers on the floor, looked at Lefty, and snorted. He gathered them into a pile, grabbed the recorder, and walked out, chuckling.

FIVE

||||||||||||||||||||||||||||||||||||||||||||||||||||||||||||||||||||||||||||||||||||||||||||||||||||||

Mary

The day before Christmas was only a half day at both work and school, so Mary left before noon to pick up Jacob. She thought they would stop somewhere for lunch, run home to change and pack, then head to the assisted-living facility to see Rick before leaving for her parents' house.

Even though she'd dropped him off just a few hours before, Mary couldn't wait to see Jacob. She pulled into a waiting space and kept her eyes on the front door of the school, not wanting to miss the moment he jogged out.

A young father and son stepped into view. The father picked the boy up. "Oh, you're getting so big!" Mary heard him say. "I can barely hold you, you're so big!"

The kid giggled and kicked as the dad launched

him into the air. *Boys are supposed to be tossed around*, Mary thought. *Boys need dads. They need moms, too. But boys need dads.* She had made Jacob laugh a few times, and they'd even wrestled a bit. But nothing like this.

It was obvious this kid had been tossed hundreds of times, because even in midair, he showed zero fear. He knew Dad was strong enough to catch him, and he looked euphoric.

Mary hadn't seen that look on Jacob in 366 days.

As father and son walked off, Jacob appeared in the doorway. He got a quick hug from Megan and trotted toward the minivan.

Mary's whole body warmed. "Hey, guy."

"Hey," he said, climbing into the backseat and buckling himself in.

"We're going to eat and then go see Daddy, right?"

"I know."

"So, you ready?"

"Yeah."

He also hadn't been too talkative in 366 days.

Eva

Not wanting to leave anything outstanding, Eva called her bank. After about ten automated voice prompts, she finally reached a real person, who of course put her on hold. She used the time to take a few of her pills, still following the "red with red and yellow with yellow" directions.

Eva fought the urge to dwell on what this day was. She remembered watching a film about a man who was on death row and how he spent a few hours in the afternoon of his last day chatting with his family before just hanging out in his cell. She'd thought about how agonizing that must be, counting the minutes until your death. The ache in your gut, the buzz in your ears that came every time you reminded yourself that this was it.

She wasn't beholden to anyone on this day. No one was forcing her to do anything like in a death row situation. But she knew today was her last day. And even though she'd prepared herself for it and had come to accept it, she understood that gut aches and ear buzzes would likely come. Guilt, fear, or sadness would creep in. But as bizarre as it sounded, she did not want to spend the whole day sad. Every time a depressing thought entered her mind, she shut it down and focused on the task at hand.

When she was finally talking with Janet in Account Services, Eva told her she wanted to close her savings account. "I'm not upset with the bank or anything. I just would like to use the money for something."

Janet chuckled. "We don't take it personally, ma'am," she said, then verified Eva's account number. "All right, Mrs. Boyle. Would you like the nine dollars and fifty-two cents sent to you there at Cornell Street?"

"Nine dollars and fifty-two cents?"

"Yes, ma'am. Are you still on Cornell?"

"Yes, but don't send it here, please. Um, send it to the Salvation Army. I'll bet they could use it, don't you think?"

"We're not able to do that, ma'am."

"That's fine. I'm sorry. I didn't mean to be a bother."

"It's okay, ma'am. So we can send it to your home?"

"Yes, thank you."

Eva decided she would leave a note asking that the money be sent to the Salvation Army. It wasn't much, but it was better than nothing, right?

Lefty

Lefty scrounged through his trunk for his six-year-old cell phone. The ridiculously large thing hadn't had service in months, but it would do.

He paced the sidewalk in front of Ed's Gas 'n' Things and waited. When a customer emerged, Lefty was suddenly in the middle of an important call.

"Yes, sir, that item is on back order right now, but we'll get it out to you as soon as we can! . . . Hello? Hello? Oh, man! Stupid phone!"

Lefty kicked the ground and gestured to the customer. "Excuse me, sir, my phone just ran out of battery. Could I borrow yours for a minute?"

The man kept walking.

Lefty resumed his position and waited. A sharply dressed professional finished pumping gas and approached.

"Yes, sir, but this deal can only close after I've seen all the important documents—Hello? Stupid phone! Sir?"

The guy actually stopped.

"Sorry to bother you, but I'm in the middle of closing a huge deal. Could I borrow your phone a minute, please?"

"What happened to *your* phone?" Professional said, reaching for Lefty's.

"Ah, it just hasn't been the same since I dropped it on my boat."

"Your boat."

"Yes, sir."

"What *is* this thing? You were using this? Just now?"

"Yes. Very important business call. Could I please use yours?"

"I guess, but for just a minute. I've got a two o'clock."

"Oh, hey, me too. Thanks."

Lefty dialed the high-tech phone and took a few steps away.

"Heather, it's me, Lefty."

"I know it's you, Lefty. What's this number?"

"A friend. Whatever." Lefty knew better than to call her collect.

"How'd the meeting go?"

"Don't act like you don't know. Your attack dogs screwed me over again. I knew this was gonna happen!"

"What are you talking about? All you had to do was sign the papers."

"That's what the court said! But your—" what little sense Lefty had left kept him from using the language he wanted to—"your jerk lawyers wouldn't let me! They said we had to set up another meeting with the judge. I'm telling you, Heather, I'm getting sick and tired of this—" Lefty checked his tongue again—"this stuff!"

"Lefty, I honestly don't know what you're talking about. Why wouldn't they let you sign the papers?"

"Because you and your new boyfriend don't want me to see the kids!"

Heather spoke slowly. "You know that's not true, as long as you're sober. We've been through this. Besides, it doesn't matter what I want. The judge said you can see them, so you can see them."

"Tell that to your lawyers!" Lefty was at full volume. Professional shuffled, looking antsy.

"Lefty, would you please calm down and tell me what happened?"

This was the tone of voice that Lefty hated—the one that dripped with parental condescension. Heather had been twenty-five when she married Lefty, who was seven years older. She was upper

middle-class from a respected family. Dad was a doc-
tor and an elder at Grace Fellowship; Mom was a college professor. Lefty knew he represented her
rejection of that life, and he was proud of it. Now she
sounded like one of them, and nothing he could say
seemed to shake her out of that state.

"All I know is they say that since I don't have an
apartment, I don't get to see the kids."

Professional stepped in. "Excuse me, but I need
my phone back."

Lefty raised a hand. "Just one minute, friend.
Thanks."

Heather sighed. "What happened to your apartment?"

"I don't want to talk about that now, so just lay
off it!"

"Whatever. What else did they say?"

"They said I couldn't see the kids. How many
times do I have to say that?"

Professional had clearly heard enough. "Excuse
me, but I really have to go."

"Just back off a minute, buddy, okay? I told you,
this is a very important business call!"

The guy backed away and entered the store.

"I'm telling you, Heather, this ain't right! And if it
doesn't get fixed, I'm gonna go off on somebody!"

"Where are you, Lefty?"

"Everything was fine, and then I slipped and told
them I got fired, and they ran out of there like bats

out of hell with their cappuccinos spilling all over themselves!"

"You got fired?"

Ah, well; she would have found out soon enough.

Suddenly a beefy, sixtyish man appeared in front of Lefty. *Ed* was sewn on his shirt, and he carried a baseball bat. He didn't need it. "Is that this gentleman's phone?" he bellowed.

"Just one second, sir." Lefty turned away. "Heather, I gotta go—"

"Yeah, you gotta go," Ed growled, ripping the phone from Lefty as Heather called out, "Are you across the street again?"

Ed shoved Lefty with the bat, sending him flying toward his car.

"What's the matter with you?" Lefty whined.

"Get outta here!"

Lefty stumbled to the safety of the other side of the car before getting in a final dig. "You've got problems!" He slammed the hood with an open hand. Ed slammed the other side with his bat.

Lefty jumped in and peeled out, sneaking a peek across the street at Heather's window. She was staring out, shaking her head.

SIX

3:00 P.M.

‖‖

Kirk

It had been a mistake to open the station today.
Since his "morning rush"—two customers—Kirk had
waited on a grand total of two more. And neither had
been in a festive enough mood to buy cranberries.

Kirk should have been depressed. He had just
cause: he hadn't had a girlfriend in ten years, his
only family consisted of a sister who lived a thousand
miles away, and he owned a rat-hole gas station with
no customers the day before Christmas.

But he didn't care enough to be depressed.

At least being stuck in this place for good had one
benefit: it relieved him of the pressure to be sad.
Years ago he'd come to accept reality, and now the
routine was so, well, routine that he was numb.

He also didn't have to feel guilty that he contrib-
uted nothing to society. He'd put in some time in the

53

charity department with his ailing mother for a few years before she passed. But there was nothing significant he could do now anyway. He had neither the time nor the opportunity.

The minutes crept by. The hum of the freezers and soda machines matched the steady, endless pattern of each day. When Kirk had to go to the bathroom, it was the first time he'd ventured more than fifteen feet from the counter all day.

Lefty

Lefty had been sitting in his car on a small dirt path off the main road for an hour. He was developing a plan.

Lefty was a loser. He knew it. It didn't take a genius to know that nothing worked in his life. He'd been dealt a bad hand, sure, but every attempt to play that hand had only made things worse.

And now, the jig was up. He had run out of people who didn't know the deal with him. Maybe his kids didn't know yet, but he wasn't going to see them anyway. He could move, but where would he go? If he applied for a job, what would he list as an address? And even if he could figure out a way to get a job, he knew the pattern would continue. He had no reason to assume that sobriety was a possibility for him or that he had the ability to hold a job for longer than two years. He could point to nothing in his past that gave him any reason to feel optimistic, and he had reached an age where forming new habits was all but impossible.

When Lefty was in high school, his church youth group had held a weekend retreat. Lefty wasn't really into church, and he'd gone only because his mom said he and his siblings had to. But retreats were usually fun.

On the retreat, the leaders had split the kids into small groups for an exercise. Each person would take a turn completing the sentence *If you really knew me, you'd know that . . .* Most revealed something intense or personal, and everyone cried and supported each other. Lefty had said, "If you really knew me, you'd know that my dad and I don't get along." He had cried. It was the only time in his life he had been hugged by several people who seemed to genuinely care about him. He'd even prayed that night, and it had felt good.

He didn't know why that was on his mind. But just ten minutes ago, he'd spoken aloud in his car.

"If you really knew me, you'd know I hate myself as much as everyone else does."

Saying it didn't make him feel better, but it made him realize he had no one to live for, including himself. It reminded him that no one needed anything from him, and he had nothing to offer other than four tubs of paint. It gave him permission to commence his plan.

It gave him permission to kill himself.

Eva

It was time for another round of pills. Eva had more to do today, so she was in no rush to mix the red with the yellow and face the end.

She didn't know if it was stress or simply old age, but even her normal pill routine was becoming increasingly difficult. Every swallow took effort. Trying to take two at once, she nearly gagged, and it took several sips of water to get them down.

She would have to be creative tonight. Nothing would be worse than a failed attempt, or even a successful attempt that resulted from choking on a handful of pills. Eva hadn't asked for much in life, but she thought she deserved a gentle, painless, and dignified death.

Dissolved pills would have the same effect as whole ones and might be easier to get down, so she figured she would mix them in hot water and drink it like tea. This would also be nice because, though an autopsy would show what she had ingested, no suicide note and no sign of distress might imply it had been an accident.

Was that a good or a bad thing? Maybe her children should know she had killed herself. Maybe they should wonder if perhaps their not visiting or writing her in years was a factor.

No. They had suffered enough. Her husband, their father, had been a bad man. No other way to put it. As Pastor Mark had said in several sermons,

🎥 MIDNIGHT CLEAR

STILL PHOTOS FROM THE MOVIE

Eva (K Callan) accepts a gift from Margaret (Victoria Jackson).

Lefty (Stephen Baldwin) in a meeting with his ex-wife's lawyers.

Mary (Mary Thornton) and Jacob (Dominic Scott Kay) in their car.

Kirk (Kirk B.R. Woller) waits during a boring day.

Eva picks up her pills.

Pastor Mark (Richard Fancy) comforts Mitch (Mitchell Jarvis).

Lefty is confronted by police officer.

Mr. K's Quick Stop in the morning.

Mitch with the carolers.

Mary and Jacob arrive at the assisted-living facility.

Jacob, Mary, and Kirk discover a surprise.

Kirk, Mary, and Jacob prepare to say good-bye.

Mitch sees a surprise guest at church.

▣ MIDNIGHT CLEAR

BEHIND-THE-SCENES PHOTOS FROM THE MOVIE

Setting up for a scene at the gas station.

Director Dallas Jenkins (seated) explains a shot.

evil and sin exist, and people aren't good at heart. Her husband wasn't good. The drinking was a major reason, sure, but he wasn't good sober, either.

She could never explain why she'd married him. It was probably the feeling that came from being liked by a man, which, because of her own emotionally dead father, she hadn't previously experienced. Once married, she hadn't believed she had a choice. Her church spoke against divorce, and she didn't have the confidence to separate, so she learned to cope.

That had probably been her biggest mistake. Perhaps divorce wasn't the answer, but she could have protected the kids better. He had never hurt any of them, but he had hurt her. And what could be worse for kids than hearing their mom get hit by their own dad?

She had done everything to serve them, but kids take that for granted anyway. She couldn't protect them from the damage that comes from having an alcoholic, emotionally abusive father.

Of her three kids, one had made a decent life for himself, but it had been intentionally independent of his family. She couldn't blame him.

So yes, she would make it look like an accident. And she would continue to tidy up the house and close her accounts, leaving everything as hassle-free as possible. It was the least she could do.

Mitch

"All right, everyone, listen up. Chad, you listening?"

Mitch stood in front of eight teenagers, all displaying respectable attempts at dressing Christmassy—at least as Christmassy as they could in shorts. At least a few of the shorts and T-shirts were green, and the occasional reindeer hat and scarf sold it. In the Southwest, this was as Christmassy as it got.

Mitch wasn't surprised that only eight had shown up. He wouldn't have when he was in high school. A couple of them were likely forced by their parents, but these were good kids.

"Now there's a rumor going around that caroling is a dorky thing to do."

The kids looked sheepish.

"Well, I'm here to tell you that, unfortunately, it's not a rumor. Caroling *is* a dorky thing to do."

They chuckled.

"So don't sweat it. We've got a few early stops to make, and I know it's going to be a long evening. But we're in this thing together, so let's make it fun, got it? You with me?"

A couple of weak *yeah*s.

"I said, 'Are you with me?'" Mitch shoved on a Santa hat for emphasis. He felt like Patton.

The response wasn't much better.

"Got it. You guys are too cool for excitement. Congrats. Come on, let's go."

Lefty

The most interesting thing about Lefty's decision to end his life was his twinge of guilt. He was normally numb to guilt. Alcohol helped. So did repetition of bad behavior.

What's more—perhaps because he had been thinking of the youth group retreat—the guilt made him think of God. He wasn't sure he believed in God, but if there was a God, He was making Lefty feel guilty about killing himself.

So Lefty tried something he hadn't done in years.

"God, it's me, Lefty. Or Luschel, if that's what You call me. If You're real, I'm sorry for being me. And all the bad and stupid stuff I've done—I'm sorry for that. And I'm sorry for killing myself. You didn't exactly give me a great life. But whatever. Please forgive me for killing myself, and please don't send me to hell if there is one."

Nothing eloquent, he knew, but it was as much as he could muster.

So now guilt could be added to the other feelings he planned to rid himself of. And wasn't that the point? To escape from all the . . . from everything?

Lefty's plan was to go to Tommy, one of his childhood friends, who now worked out of his garage and knew how to get things. Tommy would have a gun. He would also have booze, which would serve two purposes: One, it would be its usual wonderful self, which Lefty wanted as his "last meal." Two, it would medicate—camouflage fear, break down natural resistance, dull survival instinct.

But the paint in the trunk wouldn't be enough for Tommy to give up a gun and booze. Lefty needed more to trade, so he started the car, turned onto the main road, and headed out to get it.

||||||||||||||||||||||||||||||||||||||||||||||||||||||||||||||||||||||||||||||||||||||||||||||||||||||

Mary

The drive to the assisted-living facility was quiet.
This was typical. Jacob was pretty quiet at home
anyway, but whenever they went to see Rick, he was
silent. Mary had learned to just let him be.

She worked hard not to spoil him, a common
temptation when a kid experiences trauma. Adults
feel so bad for the kid that they avoid anything that
might upset him, like the discipline or structure he
needs. Mary had tried not to give in to that temptation, but she did allow Jacob his silence. He would
sort this out in his time, and she wouldn't push him.

When they pulled in, Jacob remained his seat.
"Mom? Is Daddy gonna talk to me this time?"

Mary forced a smile. "I don't know, honey. We'll see
how he feels. But I do know that we're going to tell him
that we love him. And what else are we going to say?"

"Merry Christmas?"

"That's right! Good job. Ready?"

Mary refused to sugarcoat the issues or lie to Jacob. From the moment she found out about the accident, she'd known he was too smart for that. She invented ways to distract him sometimes, sure, and she tried to maintain strength and a positive attitude. But there would be no promises that Daddy would get better, no pretending that Daddy was just feeling a little sick. When Jacob asked questions, she gave honest answers. The devastation of the situation was hard enough; she didn't want to add dashed hopes to the equation.

As they approached the entrance, Mary felt Jacob's hand slip into hers. There were times she loved him so much she could barely take it.

Eva

Eva went from room to room, vacuuming every inch of the house. Each room took three times as long as normal because she went over and over the same spots. Her thoughts were elsewhere. This was the kind of mindless task that didn't force her to concentrate on anything specific.

Eva was short for Evangeline. She'd never liked her name. She was the eldest of seven born to a farmer who'd tried to make up for his mistakes in life by giving his children spiritual or biblical names. Evangeline, Matthew, Mark, Luke, Chastity, Ruth, and Cletus, who unfortunately was born after Eva's father had gotten the godly name obsession out of his system.

Eva's parents didn't celebrate birthdays. They didn't show affection. Back in those days, kids only spoke around adults when spoken to, and that didn't happen often in her family. Her mother wasn't quite all there in the head, which only gave her father license to detach himself from the family even more. He'd had several girlfriends on the side; Eva knew of at least two because she'd caught him twice.

She had tried to reverse the cycle with her own family, but she just wasn't very good at it. She even tried saying "I love you" to her kids occasionally—something she'd never heard growing up—but her husband didn't join in, and it eventually became too awkward. The unfortunate thing was that because she didn't say it, she didn't hear it either.

These were the kinds of things she didn't want to dwell on today. She chastised herself and focused on the carpet.

Mary

"Hi, Mary! I'm glad you came in today!" Denise, the self-described bold, black, and beautiful receptionist, said with her usual huge smile. "Hey, little man, how's it goin'?"

"Merry Christmas."

Mary and Denise chuckled. "We've been working on that one," Mary said as she rubbed Jacob's head.

"I'll make sure they get Rick to the TV room, honey," Denise said, picking up the phone. "Oh, Mary . . . he had, um, a bit of an angry spell this morning. Had to be medicated again." She glanced at Jacob. "He's not going to be very lucid today."

Mary often raised a fuss at such news. She was fiercely protective of Rick, and they were supposed to let her know before they prescribed any drugs. The staff called such meds "chemical restraints," but that was just code for "drugs to shut him up." Sometimes he needed them, because an outburst might have been caused by delusions or reaction to a medicine. But if Rick's behavior was the result of his simply being tired or sore or frustrated by his inability to communicate, Mary could calm him without the drugs. And they had known she was coming today.

But this afternoon a fight wasn't worth it. Jacob was here, it was Christmas Eve, and she was about to leave Rick for a couple days. So she gave the response she had gotten used to giving when she was tired.

"Okay."

Mary and Jacob waited in the lounge. Mary's parents had money, and they supplemented Rick's insurance to keep him in a nice place like this. Nothing fancy, but it was clean and had a pleasant atmosphere. Christmas music played in the background as patients and visitors chatted.

Rick was wheeled in to a table next to Mary and Jacob. He wore sweatpants and a sweatshirt, so he looked comfortable, but his eyes barely flickered in recognition.

"Hi, baby," Mary said. "How are you?"

He stared at her.

"It's Christmas Eve, Rick. I don't know if you knew. . . . Um, Jacob is here to see you. I knew that would mean a lot to you. Say hi to Daddy, sweetie."

"Hi, Daddy." Jacob turned to Mary. "Why does he have a beard?"

"Well, I don't know. You like it?"

Jacob took another look and smiled. "Yeah, I like it." He leaned close to Rick's ear. "Merry Christmas!"

"Honey, you don't have to get that close. Daddy can hear you. He just can't show you right now because of the medicine."

"Oh."

"Hey, give Daddy a kiss and tell him you love him; then go play over there with the puzzles."

"I love you, Daddy." He kissed Rick on the cheek, then pulled back and giggled. "His beard is tickly."

With Jacob in the corner, Mary said, "He's doing really well, Rick. He's still quiet, holds it all in. But he's so polite and courteous and thoughtful. So much like you it freaks me out sometimes."

Rick just sat there, and Mary pressed her lips together.

"Oh yeah, he advanced another round in the

spelling bee this week! He and Sammy Jarvis both get to go to the district competition after New Year's. I'm going to take off work and see it."

Rick maintained her gaze but didn't respond.

Mary hung her head and sighed. "It's hard, Rick. So hard. There's no one I can really talk to about this. No one knows what to say, and then I feel weird because I know they're uncomfortable. For the first time in my life I feel alone. And I don't even know where God is in all this, you know? I'm just so numb right now. I can't even cry anymore."

She looked deep in his eyes. "I need help, Rick."

She gently wiped saliva from his chin. "I sure wish they wouldn't dope you up so much. This just isn't you."

Mary glanced at the clock on the wall. "Well, we've got to get going. We're making the drive to my parents' tonight. We'll be back in two days, and we'll spend the whole day here, okay?"

She stared at him, then suddenly grabbed his arm. "Please come back," she whispered. "I love you so much. Merry Christmas."

She kissed him and smiled. Jacob was right. Rick's beard tickled her.

An orderly wheeled Rick back to his room.

Mary needed a moment to herself, so she told Jacob he had two more minutes, then moved into the empty hallway. She was so tired of this. This was not how Christmas Eve was supposed to be celebrated, and there was nothing she could do about it.

Ironic, she thought. Most marriages in crisis still had hope if both parties were willing to work on it. She and Rick had a significant communication problem—a morbid understatement but true. They were both willing to fix it, but they couldn't. The vitality of their marriage was in the hands of modern medicine and the supernatural. And neither was doing much.

"Mary!"

Startled, she looked up to see Mitch and a few kids from his youth group lounging in the lobby. Mitch had been Rick's best friend until the accident had changed everything. She knew he still loved Rick, but it obviously drove Mitch nuts that he couldn't do anything to help.

Mary loved Mitch, and she hated that they couldn't have a normal conversation anymore. Each reminded the other of the accident, and hard as they tried, they could never ignore the elephant in the room.

"Hey, Mary, I thought I might see you here!"

"Yeah, he needs me here. I think. Have you seen him lately?"

Mitch

From early on, every time Mitch saw Mary, she asked if he'd seen Rick lately or when he would see him next. But after a while, seeing him had just gotten too hard. Couldn't she understand that?

What a ridiculous question. Of course she could understand it. It must be immeasurably harder for her than for Mitch.

"Uh, not exactly. I, uh, have a pretty full schedule now with the high schoolers and all. I do need to find some time to stop by. I just—"

"He needs to see people, Mitch. People who love him. I know it might be awkward, but it's so good for him."

Mitch couldn't miss the desperation in her eyes. Man, no wonder Rick always talked about how great his marriage was. Her love for him was fierce. "I know, Mary. You're totally right."

Jacob emerged from the lounge, and Mitch grinned, bending to greet him.

"Hey, tough guy! Merry Christmas!"

"Merry Christmas."

"Hey, man, I'm gonna come by your house sometime soon, okay?"

Jacob brightened. "And go to the swings park?"

"Yeah, that's right! We love the swings, don't we?"

"Yeah."

Mitch felt like a jerk. Why didn't he spend more time with them? Too busy to give his best friend's son a male presence in his life?

He stood. "I'm sorry I haven't been a good friend, Mary. To Rick or to you. I still don't know what to do with all this. It's not an excuse. I'm just saying I'm really sorry."

Mary nodded, looked away.

"Not that I should feel sorry for myself, of course. I was back on my feet a month after the accident. You're the one who got the bad deal."

"You got a bad deal too, Mitch. I know how close you were."

"Yeah, but I'm not stuck in a—you know, I'm going to stop talking now."

Mary smiled. "No, it's okay. I really did get a raw deal on this one, huh?"

"Hey, why don't you come to church tonight? We haven't seen you there since it happened. Tonight might be the right night for it."

"I can't, Mitch."

"Come on. I'd make sure no one made it awkward for—"

"I can't, okay? I just can't." Mary reached for Jacob, breaking eye contact.

"Well, we all love you there. You know that, right?"

"Yeah."

"Right, Mary?"

"Yes. Right. I know." She looked at Mitch pointedly. "Does everyone still love Rick?"

Ugh. Their conversations always leaned this direction. She wasn't being totally fair; the church had tried to stay active in her life, and Pastor Mark visited Rick every week. But she wasn't being totally unfair, either. It was awkward, plain and simple, and few were good at handling it. He certainly wasn't. But that was no excuse. They should get better at it.

Mary stepped closer. "I'm sorry, Mitch. I actually am really glad I saw you. I don't mean to talk like this. Let's please keep in touch, okay? And I know that tonight might be too tough, but please. See him."

Mitch nodded. "I know. I'm sorry. I know."

"Merry Christmas, Mitch." She squeezed him tight.

Mitch ruffled Jacob's hair before Mary led him away.

She turned. "Oh, and Rick has a beard now. So if you kiss him, you should know that his beard is tickly."

Jacob giggled.

Another reason Rick talked about how great his marriage was.

"They're ready for the carolers in the cafeteria," Denise called out.

Mitch led the kids down the hallway to cheer people up, something he was unqualified for at the moment. Funny how that worked.

Mary

Jacob climbed into his seat, and Mary pulled out to begin the two-hour drive to her parents' house. She felt bad about her conversation with Mitch, but it had been destined to be uncomfortable. Best friend, wife, anniversary of the accident. All in all they did okay, and it was good to see him. But once again she'd had to work to make someone else not feel awkward. Funny how that worked.

EIGHT
5:00 P.M.

||||||||||||||||||||||||||||||||||||||||||||||||||||||||||||||||||||||||||||||||||||||||||||||||||||||||||

Lefty

Lefty pressed the intercom button.

"You shouldn't be here, Lefty," Gary, head of factory security, squawked.

"Oh, hey, Gary. It's me, Lefty."

"I know it's you. Why do you think I just called you Lefty? You gotta get out of here."

"Can I just get the rest of my stuff, please? . . . Gary?"

"You mean the rest of those paint cans?"

Lefty hung his head. "Well, all right then. I'm goin' now! Bye, Gary."

Lefty slowly backed out of camera view, knowing Gary would already be drifting into his normal half-awake state.

Then Lefty hit the gas and rocketed forward,

smashing through the wooden gate. As he sped past the intercom, he heard Gary's desperate "Lefty!"

For a hollowed-out drunk, Lefty was a surprisingly deft driver, retaining most of his cruising and high school drag racing experience. He peeled around a corner and screeched to a stop in front of the storage shed. He grabbed as many assorted tools and pieces of equipment as he could and dropped them into the trunk with the paint drums.

"Lefty!" Gary's voice spun him around.

The 350-pound chief emerged from the security shack and slid into a golf cart, a mug of coffee in his hand. Gary was only twenty feet away but obviously in no mood to run. Lefty's pulse quickened as Gary floored it. The last thing he needed was to go to jail and prolong his misery. If he could just get out of here and get to Tommy's, he figured he could lie low long enough to get done what he needed to get done.

Lefty hopped into his car and took off just as Gary arrived.

"Lefty, get back here!"

Gary and the cart quickly grew smaller in Lefty's rearview mirror.

Smash!

As Lefty was about to turn onto the main road, his rear window cracked into a thousand spiderwebbed strands. He looked back to see Gary giving himself a congratulatory fist pump. The chief had hit a moving vehicle from thirty yards with a porcelain mug. Lefty was impressed.

Mitch

Rick wasn't in the cafeteria with the rest of the patients and families.

Mitch was grateful. He would visit Rick before the New Year, but tonight was not the night. He knew it would be awkward for the kids, not to mention for him, and the weight of the anniversary would make it harder than usual.

The sounds of eight teenagers stumbling through three Christmas carols mixed with the clinks of silverware to create a symphony of unpleasantness. It didn't help that one of the brain-damaged patients near the front tried to sing along. Loudly. But Mitch had to admit the people in the room seemed to enjoy it. Several of the patients' family members gave him sympathetic but reassuring looks, and they were obviously grateful that their loved ones were being given a special "program."

Was it fun? No. Embarrassing? Yes.

But it could have been worse.

Mary

As she passed through *the* intersection, Mary shuddered. It was painful every time.

She would never forget the night of the accident. Obviously.

Jacob had been in bed, and she'd been in the shower when the phone rang. After the shower, on her way to check the message, she walked past her bed and smiled; it was covered in rose petals for Rick's arrival. She checked her voice mail, and as she realized that the caller had simply hung up, she heard the doorbell ring. She quickly put on a bath-robe and approached the front door cautiously, as she always did when she and Jacob were home by themselves at night.

She would always remember the relief she felt when she saw the police officer at her door. She didn't think she needed to worry about opening it.

"Mary Franklin?"

"Yes?"

"I'm afraid your husband's been in an accident, ma'am."

After that, she didn't remember much. Several people from church had helped with Jacob and the logistics of the house, and she'd dressed and left. She stayed at the hospital for two straight days before she went home armed with some prescription sleeping pills. She had been in shock, so she hadn't cried. That is, until she slid into bed and realized it was still covered in rose petals.

Now as she drove, she thought about what she'd said to Rick tonight. *I need help.* She hadn't said that to anyone and normally wouldn't say something like that to Rick. The last thing she wanted was to make him feel guilty, but he seemed so out of it this time, she was sure it hadn't reached him.

"I need help," Mary said aloud, startling herself.

"What, Mom?"

"Nothing, sweetie. Just mumbling."

What was that? It felt like a prayer she hadn't intended. She'd just blurted it.

The engine sputtered, then stalled. Mary turned the key and it started again, but something was wrong. Lovely. Another two hundred yards and it stalled again. She steered to the side of the road.

No, no, no!

"What's wrong, Mom?"

"I don't know, honey. The car . . ." She turned the key again, whimpering, "Please."

It sputtered to life, and she got back on the road. Mary saw only fields and a lake, and she wasn't getting cell reception. She had to get to a gas station quickly. A small sign read "Gas and Groceries" and pointed past the lake.

She didn't say it this time, but she felt it. She needed help.

Lefty

Lefty's muffler scraping the asphalt announced his arrival in Tommy's driveway.

Lefty honked and Tommy's sweaty, half-shaven face appeared between the blinds, then disappeared.

The garage door slowly opened, revealing sandals, black socks, and snow-white shins.

"What?" Tommy barked.

"Whadya mean, what? I got the stuff. Give me a hand!"

"Well, don't honk, scumbag! It's Christmas Eve. I got neighbors. Back that piece of junk over here!"

Lefty had called Tommy collect, looking to trade for a gun. No surprise, Tommy claimed to have a good one. "Get here fast, and it better be worth it," he'd said.

Lefty gunned it too hard, screeching the tires and then the brakes.

"Stop screwing around, Lefty!"

"I'm not; I'm—"

"Forget it; I'm coming out. Whole neighborhood's watching anyway. Let's go."

Lefty walked to the trunk before realizing the keys were still in the ignition. He jogged back while Tommy steamed. Finally, he opened the trunk.

Tommy gave the contents a once-over. "All right, fine. Let's get the stuff into the garage."

Once inside, Tommy slammed the garage door and turned on a small overhead light.

This place never ceased to surprise Lefty. The garage looked like a RadioShack junkyard, but Tommy had catalogued every item. And he had an elaborate security system. It took a criminal to know one, apparently.

Tommy had been the kid in high school who "never applied himself" but was actually smart. He'd applied himself in shop class; other than that, it was video cameras and hustling. If Tommy had been in prison, he'd be Morgan Freeman in *The Shawshank Redemption*—the guy who could get anything. So far he'd been smart enough to avoid doing time, but he plied his trade with a client base of mostly ex-cons.

"All right, that'll work." Tommy keyed Lefty's items into an old computer, then pulled a small box from a shelf and revealed a .357 Magnum revolver. "This sucker is hot, Lefty."

"That right?" Lefty examined the piece, pretending to look for something specific.

"Scorchin'. Surprised you ain't blisterin' just touching it."

"What's with all the dramatics? We on TV?" Lefty got off a good one once in a while.

"Folks it belongs to won't be happy if they see you with it. Those folks—they wear badges; know what I'm sayin'?"

"Jeez, Tommy, where'd you get this?" Lefty felt exposed enough driving a car with a busted-up back window.

"Why don't you tell me about all this stuff, and I'll see if I can remember how I got the gun."

"I don't know. It's just a little more trouble than what I was looking for." This was Lefty's attempt at negotiating.

Tommy stared and shook his head. "It's a gun, isn't it? It goes *bang bang*. You wanna be picky, get outta here. I could care less."

Negotiation over.

"You got bullets?"

Tommy handed him a box of ammo. "Now get outta here."

"One more thing. I'm real thirsty."

"Ah, jeez." Tommy grabbed a flask of whiskey from a collection on the floor. "Now go on."

Lefty mumbled, "Merry Christmas" and walked out.

Tommy never asked or told business details. But Lefty couldn't help feeling bummed that an old high school buddy wasn't at least curious about why he wanted a weapon. He didn't know what he would have told him anyway. Certainly not the truth.

Dusk turned to darkness. 'Twas the night before.

NINE
6:30 P.M.

||||||||||||||||||||||||||||||||||||||||||||||||||||||||||||||||||||||||||||||||||||||||||||||||||||||||||||||||||||||||

Kirk

Kirk had discovered a few things about his place
during the afternoon. It had 387 ceiling tiles. There
should have been 394, but seven were missing or
damaged. Behind the counter, there were 36 floor
tiles. There were 142 items on the top shelf of the
aisle in Kirk's line of vision from the counter. And in
the last two hours, 27 cars had driven by. The evening was proving as dead as the day. He would not
be open on December 24 again; that was for sure.

Mr. K's was eerie after dark. This wasn't the most
well-lit area, so there wasn't much to see out the
window, and most of the houses were behind trees
anyway. Kirk might as well have been on an island.

He wiped down the counters for the second time
that day, then wiped vapor off the glass on the small
freezer, revealing the frozen dinners. He hadn't eaten

81

since breakfast, so this would have to do as his special Christmas Eve meal. He took a turkey and gravy box over to the microwave. Three more hours and he would go home. He had done nothing all afternoon, and he had gotten in a groove. He could do nothing for three more hours. Having no more customers would actually be nice.

On cue, the door rang, and a sixtysomething, shabby-looking man walked in. Kirk hadn't heard a car, so the guy must have been camping at the lake.

"Merry Christmas," the guy said, nodding.

"Yep."

The old man ambled to the freezer.

Kirk didn't mean to stare and usually didn't, but when you get only one customer every couple of hours, each seems more significant.

Lefty

Despite the ravages of alcohol, Lefty couldn't deny the thrill of unsacking a fresh bottle, breaking the seal by unscrewing the cap, and smelling the essence of the good stuff. And this stuff wasn't bad. Were it not that he wouldn't be here tomorrow, this whiskey was the kind of stuff that started, not ended, a binge. Funny, the booze that had nearly killed him before he could do it himself smelled almost worth living for. But he would not. It would provide a farewell hit before the farewell shot. Lefty took a swig and was instantly warmed.

He accelerated through a left turn and held the gun against the steering wheel. He wanted to load it before his senses were dulled. Lefty was usually good at multitasking while driving, but he hadn't held a gun in years. Sober or not, loading it was a challenge, and soon five bullets lay at his feet. None had made it into the gun.

Mary

Mary wasn't thrilled to be driving into this area alone with a child. She hated going to garages in *nice* parts of town. Even the decent guys were obviously thrilled to be talking to a young woman, either because they could take advantage of her lack of car knowledge or because they found her attractive. They always seemed to look at her everywhere but in her eyes. So she dreaded the prospect of asking for assistance on the outskirts of town. This was not what she'd had in mind when she involuntarily blurted out a plea for help.

As she made her way around a bend and deeper into a forested area, two mutts ran up next to the van and chased it for fifty yards. A shirtless, scrawny man stared as she drove past; he seemed just as intrigued by the fact that the car was clean as by the fact that a young woman was driving it. Three boys Jacob's age were setting off firecrackers near the road, and when Mary looked past them into the trees, she could have sworn she saw a moonshine still. Half the houses she drove past were on wheels or cinder blocks. She found herself actually wondering if being stalled on the side of the main road would have been a better option.

The car stalled again as she rounded the corner and saw the gas station. She almost blurted out a word that wasn't *help*, but she protected Jacob's ears.

The place looked empty but open.

Great. No witnesses.

Kirk

Old Man stood staring into the freezer.

"Can I help you find something?" Kirk said.

"I'm hungry."

"You've come to the right place then. You like cranberries?"

Old Man turned and stared. "Cranberries?"

"It's Christmas Eve."

The man's brow furrowed. "Do they taste different on Christmas Eve?"

"I guess not," Kirk said, chuckling. "You like turkey?" He held up his still unopened box.

"Sure, if it's not made to look like bacon or such."

Kirk was used to weird customers. He liked this guy. Why couldn't everyone be this direct? He handed him the box.

As Kirk rang up the transaction, a van rolled up near the front door. Two customers in five minutes. A rush.

The man took his bag and smiled. "Merry Christmas."

"Yep."

Kirk stared at the cranberries. *Genius.*

The man passed a young, attractive woman hurrying in. Definitely not one of the regulars.

"Do you know anything about cars?" she said, clearly desperate.

Kirk hesitated. "A little, I guess."

"Well, mine keeps stalling out on me. I've got to drive another two hours to my parents' tonight, and I don't think I'm gonna make it."

"This isn't really a garage."

"Do you know of any around here? I mean, come on, it's Christmas Eve!"

"That's the problem. Everything's closed."

"Nothing?"

"I really doubt it."

She threw her arms in the air and spun around, flipping open her cell phone.

"Reception. Finally!" She looked back toward her car, apparently making sure it hadn't been stolen.

Kirk shuffled behind the counter and stared at his feet.

"Hi, Mom. . . . No, we're still here. . . . Not home, no . . . just . . . it doesn't look like we're going to be able to make it tonight. The car is shot and I can't find anybody to fix it right now."

Kirk felt as though she sneaked a glance at him, but it could have been a guilt-induced mirage.

"Yeah, I know. . . . It's lousy, I know. But what am I supposed to do? . . . Mom, everything is closed! I can't just rent a car tonight! I'll have to see if anyone can drive out to the middle of nowhere on Christmas Eve to give me a ride back home!"

She seemed on the verge of tears. Kirk pretended to be busy.

The door rang and a young boy joined the woman.

She pulled him close. "Honey, just wait here a second. Mommy's on the phone with Grandma."

Oh, man.

Cosmic joke or not, Kirk's wish for another three quiet hours would not be fulfilled. If his sister was ever stuck like this, he hoped a guy like him would have the decency to help.

Mary

Disgusting as it usually was when a guy leered, Mary wouldn't have minded if the employee at Mr. K's had a thing for her. He didn't seem dangerous, so maybe the right look or smile would get him to help her out. Ironic. The one time a guy seemed to not even notice she was a woman, and it was when she most needed him to.

Her mom drove her nuts in situations like this. She had a knack for offering suggestions that were either impossible or obvious.

"I'll call your father. He ran out to get ice cream."

"Sure, call Dad, like he can do anything about it. You know, if you would've come down like I asked you to—"

"What about your father's back, honey?"

"Yes, I know about his back. I . . . Never mind. I'll just call you later, okay?"

"This is when I wish Rick could be with you, sweetie."

"Yes, Mom, I wish Rick were around too. I appreciate the reminder. Thanks for sharing. Bye."

Mary sighed as she snapped her phone shut. Whom could she call? Trudy had left that afternoon. Maybe Mitch would come out. He and the kids could sing to the trailer park community.

"I guess I could look at it, but—"

Mary whipped around. "What?"

The guy behind the counter mumbled, "I was just saying I could take a look at it, I guess. I mean, I really don't know much."

Mary eyed him intently. Maybe it was because she had no other options, but he really didn't seem like a threat. More shy than anything, and certainly more safe-looking than the cast of extras from *Deliverance* hanging out in the neighborhood. This was help.

"That'd be great. I mean, whatever you could do would be great." She kissed Jacob on the head and whispered, "We'll be okay, honey. Home soon."

TEN
7:00 P.M.

||||||||||||||||||||||||||||||||||||||||||||||||||||||||||||||||||||||||||||||||||||||||||||||||||||||||||

Mitch

Two elderly sisters forced smiles as Mitch and the group finished their carol and yelled, "Merry Christmas!" in unison.

"Thank you," one said as the other stared blankly, seemingly confused. "Thank you so much."

"Can we offer you a ride to church tonight?"

"That's very nice, but we need to get our sleep."

"Understood completely. How 'bout this nice gift from the youth group? One for each of you."

Gretchen, Mitch's most passionate youth grouper and the one who actually seemed to be enjoying the evening, handed the women envelopes from the festive basket.

"Well, we really don't need—"

"Oh, but we'd like you to have it. Just a reminder that you, uh, haven't been, you know, forgotten."

Mitch's earlier invitation to Mary aside, he generally hated asking people to church, especially those who had been there before. If they wanted to come, they'd come; if they didn't, why put them on the spot? Did it matter to them whether the church had forgotten them? Didn't they want to be forgotten?

As he led the kids off the porch, Mitch heard the door being double-bolted, as if the carolers might have devious plans.

"Moving right along," he muttered.

Mary

"Try starting it," the gas station guy said, still leaning under the hood.

The minivan's engine ran for a few seconds, then sputtered and died. Mary tried again—same result. She got out, Jacob in tow. She didn't want him leaving her side at this point.

The man held the air filter out to her. It looked dirty, but so did everything else under the hood.

"Is that bad?"

"Yeah, I think it's pretty bad."

"I haven't done anything to the car in a while."

"You don't say."

"Very funny. Can you fix it?"

"If I had an air filter, yeah. But I don't carry that sort of thing here. It's just a convenience store."

"That's not very convenient, now is it?"

He rolled his eyes. "I've heard that one before. A few times."

"Sorry."

The gas station guy pulled a grease-caked cap off something in the engine and groaned. "This is another problem. When was the last time you had a tune-up?"

Mary shifted. "Well, um, it would have been at least last Christmas, probably the fall before that. Rick, my husband, thought the fall tune-up would be fine for Christmas travel." *Please don't ask about Rick. Please don't.*

"You're lucky it's running at all. Plugs are trashed; the filter's disgusting. I can't imagine what the oil must look like. Last fall?"

Mary nodded.

"Why didn't you take it in after that?"

Ah, jeez. "Rick always handled things like that."

"Why did he let it go so long?"

"Well . . . that's a loaded question." She looked away, hoping he'd drop it. But why would he? She'd done everything but cartwheels to make him curious.

Kirk

This woman was obviously uncomfortable. Divorced? Why didn't she just say so? Maybe nervous he was some wacko who would stalk her if he knew she was single? He turned back to the engine, leaving an awkward silence.

"Rick was in an accident last year. He's in a home now."

Kirk turned to her, then noticed she wore a wedding ring. He should have noticed it earlier, but then, guys don't notice stuff like that. "I'm sorry."

She waved him off. "It's okay. But it left him brain damaged, and they're not sure what kind of recovery he could have, if at all, so . . ."

Kirk had no idea what to say.

She smiled. "Anyway, he hasn't been in the mood to take the car in for a tune-up this year, I can tell you that."

Kirk chuckled, unsure if he was supposed to. "I suppose you'd like to make it to your folks' place tonight, huh?"

"If we could, yeah, that'd be amazing."

"Okay, I have a plan. No guarantees, because I'm telling you, I really don't know much."

"I appreciate your even trying. I do."

"Well, we can jury-rig the points and plugs, clean up the cap, change the oil. I do have oil here; how convenient is that?"

That made her smile, and she looked relieved or at least hopeful.

"I'll use the air pump to blow out this filter, and maybe we can get by without a new one. If all goes well—and that's a huge *if*—we'll have you on the road in a couple of hours."

Mary

Either this guy knew what he was doing, or he was a really good scam artist. She wouldn't let her guard down or let Jacob out of her sight, but she sensed the man was okay.

It struck Mary that when she'd first said she needed help, it was before anything went wrong with the car. Her involuntary plea had turned out to be some sort of a preemptive strike. But she'd take what she could get.

"I don't have to have a clue what you just said," she said. "Do I?"

"Not if I don't." He smiled. "I'll show you what to do."

She looked at his name tag and offered her hand. "Kirk, right?"

"Yep."

"I'm Mary. And this is Jacob."

"Hi, Jacob." They shook hands.

Mary nudged Jacob toward the minivan's backseat. "Why don't you go read your book, hon?"

Waiting at a run-down gas station in the middle of nowhere—one miserable way to spend Christmas Eve.

But it was better than last year.

Eva

As she dusted, Eva couldn't help but associate memories with each knickknack. She came across birthday cards, an antique sewing machine, even a *TV Guide* from 1988. Each reminded her of something or someone.

The birthday cards were mostly from the church she used to attend. The sewing machine was the only thing she'd asked for when her siblings were dividing up her late mother's possessions, because one of her favorite memories of childhood was lying on the floor while she listened to the sounds of her mother mending the few articles of clothing they owned. Bill Cosby was on the cover of the *TV Guide*, and she'd never missed an episode of *The Cosby Show* since its debut.

She had never been emotional, though nostalgia had invaded in spurts over the past few months as she'd decided to end her life. Now her life seemed to be flashing before her eyes. Fortunately, her memories were doing nothing to change her mind.

A knock at the door.

What in the world?

Eva glanced through the window to find a fiftyish woman wearing jingle bell earrings and a sweater that screamed "Christmas." She stood there smiling, holding a box.

"Mrs. Boyle?"

"I'm Mrs. Boyle, and you are . . . ?"

"My name is Margaret, and I'm with Meals on Wheels!"

Eva opened the door, leaving the chain lock connected. "I can't really afford to give anything this year."

"Oh no, I'm not here to collect money. I'm here with your Christmas dinner. Merry Christmas!" Her huge smile never wavered.

"Oh, I—why are you doing that?"

"Well, because it's Christmas Eve."

"I understand; it's just that I didn't ask for—"

"Your name was given to us. We bring meals to people who may, um, may need a little extra, you know, assistance."

"I'm sorry, there's been a mix-up. I don't need a meal and I don't need assistance. Please take the meal to someone who needs it."

"Are you saying that you already prepared a meal?"

"No, I'm saying I don't need a meal. How did you get my name?"

Margaret set the box down and pulled out a piece of paper. "Well, I'm not really supposed to say, but it says here that a Dr. Lindell from the Jefferson County Walk-In Clinic—he's your sponsor. It says you told him you had six coming for Christmas dinner. True?"

Wow. Eva had just been making conversation. No one knew her family situation.

"Oh yes, I did talk to Dr. Lindell; yes, I did."

"So they *are* coming for dinner?"

"Hmm? Oh. Yes, yes, they are."

Margaret looked relieved. "Well, I guess Dr. Lindell just thought he'd help you out, then. I mean, six people!"

"Okay then, come on in. That'd be fine." Eva unhooked the chain and led Margaret to the kitchen.

"Whew, I was starting to wonder if maybe we should send Dr. Lindell in for a checkup!"

"Oh no," Eva said, chuckling. "I don't think he needs that."

"Now, this turkey should be warm for another couple of hours, so if the dinner's tonight, you'll be fine. Otherwise, you can reheat it in the morning. Same with the other dishes."

"Thank you so much."

"And when you're done, just toss the containers."

Eva wouldn't have been surprised if Margaret had cooked these meals herself. Her house hadn't seen this kind of energy or smile size in years.

Eva tried to match it. "Oh, that's nice! Well, thank you so very much for this lovely meal. I'm sure my family will be delighted! They'll think I'm a wonderful cook!"

Margaret laughed. "Well, I hope so!" She put a hand on Eva's shoulder. "And, Mrs. Boyle, you have nothing to be ashamed of."

Eva froze. Did she know something? "What do you mean?"

Margaret smiled. "You've cooked enough meals in your life. You can take a break now."

"Oh. Yes, well, I think I will take a break tonight."
Isn't that the truth!

"Well, I'm glad."

Margaret leaned in and, surprising Eva, hugged her tight. The last time Eva had been hugged like that was the last time she'd been at church. Margaret whispered, "Merry Christmas" and left humming "Joy to the World."

Eva closed the door behind her, alone with food for seven people.

Eva had hoped Margaret would leave as soon as possible, and she had stayed only a little more than three minutes. Eva already missed her.

ELEVEN

7:30 P.M.

||||||||||||||||||||||||||||||||||||||||||||||||||||||||||||||||||||||||||||||||||||||||||||||||||||||||||||||||||||||||||||||||||

Lefty

The glow of the streetlights widened, and the sounds of the outside world grew duller. The liquor was taking effect. Lefty sped around a corner and down a dark road through some trees. He wanted one last look at the town from his favorite perch at Lovers' Lane. No one would be there on Christmas Eve, right?

Wrong. Several had the same idea.

Lefty pulled into an empty spot in a long line of cars with fogged windows. His engine was barely surviving on fumes. But that was all right. This would be his final destination.

Guns had an energy to them, even just lying there. He fingered the .357. It was heavy. He had finally gotten four bullets into it, but he hoped he wouldn't need more than one. Obviously.

Suddenly visions scared Lefty. He saw himself with the gun, terrorizing the people who'd embarrassed or angered him today. His boss Dale, the snooty lawyers, Cell Phone Guy, and Gary the security guard, all pleaded for their lives as he fired. He winced at the image of his kids huddled with Heather while he threatened her boyfriend. He was intimidating, a feeling he'd always coveted, but it was ugly now.

Was he capable of violence? What if he'd had a gun during past binges? What if he survived tonight and still had the gun? The images frightened him, but they didn't seem far-fetched. He needed to end his life before he hurt someone.

A figure loomed outside, tapping on his window. Lefty jumped and slid the gun under his leg. With light nearly blinding him, he squinted to make out the thick belt of a cop. He rolled down the window.

"You all right, buddy? You alone in there?"

"Just me."

"What are you, some kind of pervert? Get your thrills doing this?"

"What do you mean, thrills?"

"I'm gonna have to ask you to leave the area."

"Is there a problem, Officer?"

"You got ten seconds or we go for a ride in my car. It's up to you."

Lefty thought of storming out of the car. He thought of asking if peeking into parked cars was how the cop got *his* thrills. He even thought of pulling the .357 from under his leg and taking the cop with him in a blaze of glory. But, as usual—

"Yes, sir." Lefty peeled out.

Kirk

It was awkward to work with Mary watching, but at least she didn't try to make small talk. She seemed available if he needed help and, to her credit, fine with silence. Kirk worked as quickly as possible, sure Mary wasn't any more comfortable than he was. He didn't want to chat, he didn't want payment, and he didn't want drawn-out thank-yous. She was in a bind, and he was doing what he could to help—his little version of Christmas spirit.

"Mom?"

Kirk, startled by Jacob's voice, stood quickly, forgetting he was under the hood. Good thing this whole situation wasn't awkward.

Mary seemed to be stifling a chuckle. "Ouch! Kirk, are you okay?"

Kirk laughed and rubbed his head. "Fine, thanks."

"Mom, I have to go to the bathroom."

Mary looked expectantly at Kirk.

Mr. K's wasn't the most kid-friendly place in the area, and even if it were, that wouldn't be saying much. "It's not exactly homey."

"I don't think Jacob will mind if you don't."

"Uh, okay. It's inside in the back. You can use it, but—okay."

Mary smiled. "Jacob, what do we say?"

"Merry Christmas!"

She laughed. "That too. What else?"

"Oh. Thank you."

Kirk needed a break himself. He hung his worker's lamp on the hood and stepped inside to get a drink.

Lefty

The dark road was quiet, so Lefty just pulled off to the side. He didn't know how his car had lasted this long on so little gas.

It was time.

He took another swig to calm his nerves. The gun felt heavier each time he hefted it, no doubt because of the alcohol.

No cars in sight. Did it even matter? Who was he hiding from? It wasn't like he could get punished for this.

He pressed the gun under his chin.

Would anyone miss him? Who would attend his funeral? Would anyone feel guilty?

Nah. It wasn't like anyone had wronged him.

His kids would be upset, but in the long run, this would be better for them. There wouldn't be any confusion or awkwardness down the road when they got a stepdad.

Jerry B. Jenkins & Dallas Jenkins

His mom. She would be upset, but she hadn't seen him in years anyway. Same with his brother and sister.

No one would be that bothered, no one would feel guilty, and eventually, no one would miss him. No reasons not to pull the trigger.

Come on, Lefty.

He took a breath and steadied himself. There wouldn't be any pain, right? Of course not. *One. Two. Three.*

He set down the gun and swigged the last of the liquor. Newly warmed, he grabbed the gun and quickly pressed the cold steel under his chin again. Didn't want to give himself time to change his mind this time. He laid his finger against the trigger.

Wait.

No! He didn't want to wait. He wasn't going to talk himself out of this one. He sucked in a breath, steadied himself again.

Wait.

Lefty dropped the gun and burst into tears. He couldn't succeed even at this! He needed more booze. Of course, the fact that he needed to be stone-cold drunk to succeed at something only confirmed his decision to go through with this. If he could coax just a few more miles out of his fuel tank, maybe he could sneak some liquor out of a gas station, finish loosening himself up, and get this done.

Mitch

The routines were the same, along with the responses. One by one, the old folks faked smiles, thanked the teens for their singing and for their gift, declined the offer of a ride to church, and said good night. The kids weren't complaining, but it was obvious the pattern was getting old.

With each house, Mitch grew increasingly restless. It wasn't about boredom. He was willing to do boring tasks, and as much as he made fun of it, he didn't mind doing stuff that was cheesy. It was about meaning. What was the lesson here? They were trying to serve these people, and none of them seemed to care. Shouldn't they be able to see some sort of payoff?

Mitch had tried to get the kids enthusiastic about the evening, and he tried to follow Pastor Mark's lead about showing them a "faith that's strong enough to make them want to do things they wouldn't normally do." But he didn't believe in it himself, and he didn't know how to fake it. This was Christmas Eve, supposedly one of the most joyous days of the year, and he would rather be anywhere but here.

Rick would have come up with some way to make this fun and different, but Mitch had nothing. He was increasingly unsure that he should even stick around as a youth pastor.

Mitch was glad to see that there was only one envelope left in the basket.

Lefty

Mr. K's appeared around a corner and Lefty pulled
in. He figured he could get inside, slip a bottle under
his jacket, use his last sixty cents for a pack of gum
or whatever, and get out of there. His plan to sneak a
gallon of gas from the pump was derailed by the Prepay Only sign.

A van sat outside with its hood raised, but there
didn't seem to be any customers to worry about.
Quick and easy, no big deal. Lefty stuffed the gun in
his pants. He wouldn't use it, but he loved the feel of
it. He was officially "carrying," and that made him
more powerful than anyone around. He deserved that
feeling for his last few moments on earth, didn't he?

As he walked in, the bright fluorescent lights
wreaked havoc on his buzzed head. The clerk moved
from the soda machine to behind the counter, eyeing
him. Lefty looked away, pretending to be focused,
and headed toward the back.

Kirk

Eight years in a low-level business in an area like
this had given Kirk excellent radar for guys up to no
good. He'd faced only one robbery attempt, but the
moron had been so tweaked out on crystal meth that
he could barely hold his gun. Kirk had been more
amused than scared. When the scrawny, shirtless
guy leaned over the counter, Kirk had grabbed his
gun and socked him in the nose at the same time.

Kirk was sure he'd had a few minor items shop-lifted over the years, but recognizing when a customer was trouble allowed him to head off most problems before they started.

The guy hanging around the liquor in the back was no good. Something about him wasn't right. Sipping his Coke, Kirk never took his eyes off him. The guy looked nervous and obviously not sober. He pulled a bottle off the shelf, looked around, then turned away from Kirk and hunched over.

Was this guy serious? Did he really think Kirk wouldn't notice?

"Can I help you find something?" Kirk said with authority.

The man jumped and quickly put the bottle back on the shelf. Kirk forced himself to keep from smiling as the "customer" approached. This guy was pathetic.

"Pump two." He pulled a dirty credit card from his pocket and slid it to Kirk.

"How much?"

"Uh, whatever. Ten bucks."

Mm-hmm.

Mary

Mary walked Jacob from the bathroom to the candy aisle. He'd been so good.

So far, the time here had been okay. Kirk was quiet but nice enough, obviously not dangerous, and

106

Jacob seemed content to read. She had noticed a small TV in the back, so she thought she'd ask Kirk if Jacob could watch it to help the time go faster if he got bored.

They would probably be back on the road soon. They would be okay.

Lefty

This was more than Lefty had bargained for. This clerk wasn't going to let him get away with anything. He was the only customer in the store and couldn't go unnoticed. And his credit card hadn't been in good standing for a month.

The man with *Kirk* on his shirt ran the card through. The way Lefty figured it, he had three choices: apologize and buy some gum, leave now, or pull out the weapon pressed against his waist. He wouldn't really use it. He didn't want to kill anyone but himself. But he could scare the guy, tell him he wanted just one bottle of liquor and two bucks' worth of gas. Would it be that big a deal? It was wrong, but he would be inflicting his own punishment in five minutes.

What if the guy had a gun himself? Heck, that wouldn't be bad. Maybe Kirk could accomplish what Lefty couldn't.

The credit card machine beeped. Kirk frowned and ran the card through again.

The time was now. Lefty lifted his shirt and

pressed his shaking hand on the gun. *Come on, no big deal. I won't hurt the guy.* He looked left and right, then behind him.

In the corner of his eye, movement. Someone, then another. Lefty quickly let his shirt slip down over the gun.

From twenty feet away, a little boy stared at him. A woman squatted near the kid, picking through the candy.

The boy smiled. "Merry Christmas."

TWELVE
8:30 P.M.

|||||||||||||||||||||||||||||||||||||||||||||||||||||||||||||||||||||||||||||||||||||||||||||||||||||||||

Mary

When Jacob said, "Merry Christmas," Mary was surprised to see he wasn't looking at her. At the register, a shoddy, middle-aged man was staring at Jacob. Normally she'd be alarmed, but he looked more shy and intimidated than dangerous.

"Mom, I said, 'Merry Christmas' to the man."

"You did? That's very nice." She nodded at the man. "Merry Christmas."

He looked surprised, as if Mary were talking to someone else. She chuckled. Who else could she be talking to?

She handed Jacob a big candy cane. "Hey, look what I got for you. Merry Christmas!"

Jacob giggled and gave her a genuine thank-you. They were stuck in a gas station on Christmas Eve, and Jacob's treat was candy off the shelf, yet he

109

seemed thrilled. It made Mary love him even more. She rubbed his head and kissed him and felt his arm wrap around her.

Lefty

Lefty stood frozen, staring at mother and son hugging each other. They were the only two people to smile at him all day and certainly the first to wish him a merry Christmas. When he was this kid's age, his mother had sometimes hugged him like that—before he got old enough to be a loser, and especially when his dad wasn't around. And the way this woman said, "Merry Christmas" to her son—so sincere and affectionate . . . Lefty hadn't heard that in ages.

His mom wasn't all bad. Annoying at times, yes, but not mean or stupid. Lefty didn't even know why he hadn't seen her in so long. It seemed whenever they got together, she would harp on him about something and an argument eventually started. But it was never unbearable.

They'd probably had a fight, he had quit talking to her for a few weeks, and then it had just grown. And once you haven't talked to someone for a while, you know the first time you do will be that much more awkward.

But he had no solid reason to have avoided his mother for years. Maybe he owed her at least a last hello and good-bye. Maybe she would be happy to see him. Maybe *she* would wish him a merry Christmas. Worth a shot. She didn't live that far away.

One thing was sure. He wasn't pulling a gun on these people.

Kirk

Little surprise, Kirk received a "Please keep card" message on his machine, so the card was either stolen or overdrawn. He tried to remain polite in these situations so as not to embarrass or anger the customer. This was especially relevant now.

"Look, sir, do you have another—?"

But when he looked up, the guy was gone, the door closing. The car peeled out. At least there hadn't been an incident with Mary and Jacob in the store.

Mary shrugged.

"Okay," Kirk said, "whatever that was—we've got work to do."

"Yes, we do. Oh, Kirk—does that TV in the back actually get reception?"

Moments later, Jacob was on a folding chair, the TV was on a couple of boxes, and the sounds of *A Christmas Carol* drifted through Mr. K's.

Lefty

As Lefty drove away, he realized he had come close to pulling a gun on the clerk. That would have scared the kid to death, and his mother too. What was he thinking? There was probably a security camera in there, and the story of a suicidal man who had first held up a gas station would have been all over the news. That's what he wanted his kids to deal with?

No, this was better. He knew how his night would end. That hadn't changed. In the meantime, he had to avoid things getting messy. Thankfully, the kid had caught his attention.

What might happen if and when he got to his mom's house? He hoped the alcohol would keep him from chickening out. Just a quick in and out, no big deal.

Eva

Eva freshened up, lit a few candles, heated all the food, and spread the big turkey dinner on the table. She thought it might be a pleasant, relaxing meal. But sitting alone at one end of the table, she found she wasn't hungry, and the size of the feast depressed her.

Eva allowed herself to dream of the few times her whole family had enjoyed a meal together— when the kids were young, before her husband got too bad. Eva had grown up on a farm, so she could cook, and she'd loved seeing her family flush with pleasure as they enjoyed her food. But as the kids got older and things got worse, meals were often fraught with tension.

She stopped herself, refusing to dwell on the bad.

Taking a small bite of turkey, she noticed the painting on her wall. *The Last Supper.* Perfect.

She waved a forkful toward the disciples. "Any of you boys hungry?"

They weren't.

Eva cleared the table and put the food in the fridge, along with the cooking instructions from Meals on Wheels. Who knew? Maybe someone could use it.

The house was clean. Eva had eaten. Nothing left to do.

Kirk

As Kirk cleaned the rotator cap, Mary stood watching him. He noticed that she also kept an eye on her son. Like before, Kirk didn't mind the silence, but Mary soon broke it.

"You're a godsend."

"No one's ever accused me of that, but let's see if I can fix your car first."

More silence.

"So what about you?" Mary said finally. "Why are you open today instead of being with your family?"

"Pretty pitiful, huh? The short answer is I've got nothing better to do."

"Oh, come on. A nice, good-looking—sorry."

"That's fine." Kirk knew she meant nothing by it. He didn't need an explanation or an apology. He just wanted the conversation over.

Mary

Oh no.

Mary had just been trying to be nice, and now she had crossed a line. Her mind raced to explain that she had no interest, she loved her husband, she wasn't flirting. Kirk hadn't even looked up, but still she was humiliated.

The fact was, she and Rick had had a fun, dynamic marriage. The stereotype of the boring Christian couple with a dull sex life hardly applied to Mary and Rick.

It had been a year since Mary had been intimate with Rick, but she barely noticed men anymore. She was a different person with different priorities. Of course she missed Rick, and perhaps one day they would be intimate again. Until then, it was Rick she wanted. Period. And she wanted everyone to know that.

"Look, I'm not implying anything here, but I want to be up front with you. I have a husband."

Kirk finally looked up. "Uh, yeah. You told me that already, remember?"

"Yeah." A long pause. "That was awkward, wasn't it? I'm sorry."

"No, of course not. I understand. I haven't been hitting on you, by the way."

"Oh, I know. And I'm sorry."

"Don't sweat it," Kirk said. "I just wanted you to know that I haven't been hitting on you."

Mary nodded and looked away.

Kirk went back to the engine.

"I'll go make sure Jacob's fine."

At least it was out in the open. She wasn't available, he wasn't interested anyway, and the night could proceed normally. Well, as normally as this night could proceed.

Eva

Red with red, yellow with yellow. So obviously, yellow with red was not good.

Eva boiled water while she poured a full bottle of yellow pills onto a glass plate, followed by a full bottle of red pills. As she prepared to tip the pills into the boiling pot, a loud knock at the door jolted her, and the plate slipped from her fingers and shattered on the floor. While teenage voices belted out "Silent Night," Eva dropped to her knees to pick up some of the pieces so she wouldn't step on them with her bare feet. She winced as a shard sliced the tip of her finger.

Knock, knock, knock!

"I'll be there in a minute!"

She stepped over the glass. Her finger wasn't bad, but it was bleeding, so she grabbed a paper towel on her way out of the kitchen.

A young man peeked through the window in the front door as he sang with some kids.

Oh, brother.

THIRTEEN
9:30 P.M.

||||||||||||||||||||||||||||||||||||||||||||||||||||||||||||||||||||||||||||||||||||||||||||||||||||||

Mitch

Last stop of the night. Thank the Lord.

As the kids wrapped up their rendition of "Silent Night," Mitch actually hoped no one was home. The house was dark except for the kitchen, but through the window he spotted the old woman moving slowly toward the door. All right, one more quick exchange and they'd be done.

When she unlatched the chain and opened the door, everyone yelled, "Merry Christmas!"

"Thank you all so much. I'm sorry, I would have had cookies, but my grandkids ate all—"

"Oh, please don't worry about that. We just wanted to stop by, tell you we've missed you at church," Mitch said.

"I've been traveling. Kids are all spread out, you know."

"Really?" Mitch double-checked his notes, which read, *Shut-in, rarely leaves the house.*

He looked back up at the woman. "Will we see you at the service tonight? Eleven o'clock sharp. Well, give or take." He chuckled. "We can come by and pick you up."

"I'm afraid not. Got my whole family coming tomorrow."

"Okay, maybe next week then." Mitch noticed a paper towel speckled with blood wrapped around her finger. She quickly covered it. No wonder she seemed nervous and distracted. He'd give her some space.

"Well, you take care of yourself. And merry Christmas!"

She said, "Merry Christmas" and flashed an obviously fake smile as she shut the door and locked it.

The kids trudged off the porch as Mitch checked Eva Boyle off his clipboard. He called out, "Zero for seven, but the singing got better!"

"Really?" Gretchen said, still bubbling as she hopped down the porch steps.

"No, but these people probably can't hear it anyway."

"The packet! You forgot to give her the packet."

"The packet. You know, I don't think she really—"

"Oh, come on. She might need it. That's what it's for."

Mitch couldn't say, "Well, Gretchen, I'm only doing this to obey my pastor, and he won't know the difference if we just toss this last packet."

He told the students to hold on and jogged back to the door.

Eva

Eva was in the kitchen and about to wash her finger when she heard knocking again. This was getting ridiculous. She hadn't had this many people at her door in months, and they didn't even know her. It was as if someone had heard what she was planning to do tonight and was sending a bunch of people to distract her.

She unlocked and opened the door again, this time not even forcing a smile. The group leader stood alone, smiling. What could this guy want now?

"Yes?"

"I nearly forgot. A gift from the youth group." He held out an envelope.

"I really don't need anything."

"It's just a small something. To let you know how much you're loved and, uh, missed at the church."

He glanced at her paper towel again as she took the envelope.

Please, no questions. Just leave. "Well, thank you very much." Eva started to close the door.

Mitch

Was she just nervous around people, or was something wrong? Mitch wasn't thrilled with his task, but neither was he heartless. He couldn't justify leaving if something was really wrong. He took off his hat. "Are you okay?"

"I'm fine." Back came her fake smile.

"Are you sure? Is there anything I can—?"

"No. Please. I'm fine."

"All right." He looked in her sad eyes. "Merry Christmas."

"Merry Christmas." And she was gone again.

Eva

Finally.

Did the young man really mean it? Did they miss her at the church? Maybe, but it didn't matter. She had enjoyed that church for years and occasionally missed the company of some of the ladies from Sunday school and Bible studies. But as she got older and it became more difficult to get there, her heart just hadn't been in it. She knew she could have decent friends if she returned, but she wasn't *needed* there. And that was what she really longed for: to know she was needed.

Eva turned on a lamp in the living room. The stress of the visit compelled her to sit. She opened the envelope and pulled out a note and a CD titled *Songs for a White Christmas.*

Ha. Not in this part of the country.

Eva, this is just a small token from us on
Christmas. Hope it's of some use to you. We miss
you at Grace Fellowship.

    God bless,

    Pastor Mark Russell

That was nice. The token was a twenty-dollar bill.
Eva chuckled at the irony. Not much she could do
with twenty bucks the last night of her life. Guess
the Salvation Army would get twenty-nine dollars
and fifty-two cents this year. She laughed, then
laughed harder, finally bursting into sobs.

Eva wasn't sure why she was crying. She wasn't
sad, really. Oh, who was she kidding? She was sad.
It was okay to admit that to herself. But the crying
felt like a final release of tension, and it felt good.
She leaned back in her chair.

Mitch

"You all right, Mitch?" Gretchen said as he joined the
teens in the van.

"Yeah, I'm fine. We're gonna call it a night, guys."

Eva Boyle's obvious discomfort had put a cap on
an already depressing evening. The kids had been
fine, but it all felt like such a waste of time. Mitch
lacked the passion to turn the evening into anything
special or convince the kids that the outing had
value.

And for a youth pastor, that was the kiss of death.

Mary

Mary sat on the pavement as Kirk worked under the hood. The moment she'd spent inside with Jacob had given her a break from the awkwardness with Kirk, but it would have been rude to leave him alone to work on her car.

Kirk looked up. "So tell me more about your husband. What does he do?"

Mary smiled. "Well, nothing."

"Yeah, I . . . yeah. What *did* he do?"

Most people talked to Mary only about Rick's state *after* the accident—her least favorite season of their marriage.

"Wow. What didn't Rick do? When we were first married, he was an engineer. He was good at it too, got promoted several times. He always joked that he'd never stop until he built the perfect mousetrap. Then one day he comes home and tells me he's quitting."

"Just like that?"

"Just like that. And he did. Next thing I know he's working at a ranch for at-risk kids. Helped run it year-round."

"Wow. Talk about a pay cut."

"Yeah. Most of the kids had the choice of going to the ranch or going to juvie. Often he'd come home with black eyes, cuts, bruises, but he loved it. He loved those kids. He also volunteered at our church, mostly with the youth group."

In the past year, Mary had developed a habit of keeping her hands in her pockets or tucked under opposite arms. But she noticed now that her hands were out and open as she pumped Rick up to someone who didn't know him. It reminded her of why she'd fallen in love with him in the first place.

Why didn't more people talk with her about Rick? They probably thought she'd feel uncomfortable, but they were wrong. This was euphoric.

"Busy guy," Kirk said.

"Yeah, he'd help anyone who needed it."

"Jeez, sounds like a real jerk."

Mary smiled and looked away.

"That was supposed to be a joke," Kirk said. "I'm sorry. That was stupid."

"I know; it's fine. It's just that he can't help anyone now. Like his purpose has been taken away, you know?"

Kirk continued working. For a moment, it appeared he wanted to say something but was stopping himself. Then he looked up. "My mom had a stroke in the later part of her life. She couldn't take care of herself anymore."

"I'm sorry. So you know what it's like."

Kirk straightened and leaned on the side of the car, facing Mary. "It wasn't quite the same as what you and your husband are going through, but my sister and I did have to take care of her. My dad . . . he couldn't handle it, I guess."

"Yeah. A lot of people can't."

Kirk paused. This was obviously uncomfortable for him, and he made little eye contact, but he seemed determined to make his point. "It's funny, though. I'm grateful for that time."

"How so?"

"Well, it's easy to take care of someone who can give back or say thank you. But taking care of someone who can't say it, who may not always even know what you're doing—it makes you see what kind of a person you really are, you know?"

"Huh."

"I mean, I'm not saying that's why this stuff happens. That's just what I got out of it."

"Yeah, I wish other people saw it that way. They feel awkward; they don't know how to talk to him or even about him. Other than the pastor of my old church, no one visits him regularly." Mary looked down. "I'm embarrassed for him."

She hadn't admitted that to anyone. Maybe she felt free to now because she wasn't likely to ever see Kirk again, or maybe it was that he probably understood. She hadn't been able to tell her friends how embarrassing it was to get sympathetic looks from people she knew when she took Rick for walks, how it felt to see the double takes from strangers when he acted like a child. She knew that if Rick were aware, he would be horrified at how people pitied him.

But Kirk was right. This was teaching her more about herself than anything she'd ever been through. She was tough as nails, and she was good at taking care of Rick. She hadn't given herself a chance to think about that.

It didn't fix things, of course. But since she'd noticed her hands were out and open, she hadn't felt an urge to put them back in her pockets or under her arms.

Kirk

Kirk hadn't talked about his mom in years. Maybe he could now because he wouldn't likely see Mary again or because she seemed to understand. Up until now, he'd kept from talking about her. He'd feared Mary might find it trivial, but she seemed to appreciate the story.

"Well, that was unexpected," Mary said, chuckling.

"What's that?"

"Nothing, I just—"

Kirk smiled. "Didn't expect to have a meaningful conversation with the gas station guy, huh?"

"It's not that. It's—"

"It's okay. I understand." He glanced at his store. "I know what this place looks like. I'm not proud of it."

"So then what are you doing here?"

Good question. He'd almost forgotten himself.

"When I bought it, I was a genius. The city limits were headed this way. I was going to fix it up, sell it, reinvest, make a fortune. Problem was, the city never made it, and I got stuck here. But I was already trying to make this a different kind of place, you know? A destination. Gourmet coffee, good food, great service, clean as I could get it. Thing was, I did all that, and no one gave a rip. This was never going to be a destination for anyone; it's just a stop along the way."

Probably more information than she'd asked for. He mumbled, "I don't know" and leaned back under the hood. From the corner of his eye, he saw Mary looking at him as if he might have more to say. Well, if she didn't mind . . .

"You think about that one thing you can contribute, you know? What's my thing? That I make a good pot of coffee? My customers don't really care about gourmet coffee anyway. They want gas and a Styrofoam cup full of pennies by the cash register. That's about it."

He was done. This was not a pity party. His problems didn't compare to hers anyway. But to talk about them, to say it out loud to someone who actually seemed interested, even if she couldn't do anything about it, relaxed him.

It was silent for a few moments, Mary sitting, Kirk standing at the hood of the car, pretending to look at the engine. Silence was nothing new at his place, but for the first time in ages, Kirk actually heard the night sounds of the area. He even noticed how clear the sky was and that he could see nearly every star imaginable. He'd been in a fog for so long that he couldn't remember the last time he'd realized how cool the sky looked on a Southwestern evening.

And all this because of the engine trouble of a stranger's car.

FOURTEEN
10:00 P.M.

||||||||||||||||||||||||||||||||||||||||||||||||||||||||||||||||||||||||||||||||||||||||||||||||||||||||||||

Eva

Pills and plate shards covered the kitchen floor. Eva
removed the CD from its case and slipped it and the
twenty into her pocket. She swept the shards into
the trash and used the CD case to scoop up the pills.
She rummaged for an ancient jar of bouillon cubes,
surely stale despite their individual wrappings. After
getting the water boiling again, she crumbled two
cubes into the pot. Sure enough, they were brittle
and dry as dust. But all she wanted was the salty
beef taste. She dumped the pills into the brew and
slowly stirred.

Lefty

Lefty made his way through the old neighborhood
toward his childhood home, still unsure what he
might do when he got there. His stomach tightened,

and he wondered if he'd be able to go through with it. Could he just say hi and merry Christmas, hoping to hear the same, and then be on his way? How weird would that be?

Kirk

"Tonight's the anniversary."

Kirk stopped working and looked at Mary, who was staring off into space.

"Of the accident?" he said.

"Yeah."

"Oh, wow."

"Yeah." She turned back to Kirk. "He was a good man—*is* a good man. But he was a good man. I still love him so much. I meant what I said in my vows, you know? For better or worse. All of it."

"Yeah."

"I mean, it's made me wonder who I married. Did I marry his body or his mind or his soul, you know?" Mary sighed, then buried her face in her hands.

Kirk had no idea what to do. Should he sit next to her, or would that cross a line? He wasn't used to this.

"Are, um . . . are you okay?"

She looked up quickly, smoothing her hair. "Yeah, sorry. It's just that I haven't had a chance to breathe in a while. Between fighting for Rick, staying strong for Jacob, dealing with friends—I haven't even cried in months."

Maybe that was it, Kirk thought. She needed to cry. He looked in at Jacob; the boy was still concentrating on the TV. Kirk grabbed some paper towels from the windshield-cleaner box and approached Mary.

Mary

She didn't want to make things more awkward for Kirk. She looked away, took a breath, and held back tears. She would not cry in front of him and put him on the spot. Plus, Jacob would worry.

Lost in thought, she didn't notice Kirk until his shadow covered her. She accepted a handful of blue paper towels as Kirk walked inside. Jacob still hadn't looked away from the TV, and Kirk was moving to the back of the store. Mary would have some moments to herself. Alone outside a gas station in the middle of nowhere, surrounded by trees and trailer homes.

The stress of the evening and the sweetness of Kirk's gesture were too much to bear. Mary pressed the thick paper to her face and burst into tears. Months of tension and anger and loneliness poured from her, and she was helpless to control it. And it felt so good it made her cry all the more.

Mitch

Grace Fellowship was buzzing as the service drew near. Choir members, pageant performers, and staff had arrived early, and ushers were already directing traffic, in the parking lot and inside.

Mitch and the teens came in through the back, and Pastor Mark appeared.

"Hey, guys, welcome back! Brett, Gretchen—how was it?"

"Not bad."

"It was cool."

"Good to hear."

These were good kids; Mitch could never deny that. He just wasn't sure he was fit to lead them.

"All right, everyone," he said, "head on in. Bathroom break, then free time until the service." Mitch pointed them to the youth room, and as they moved on, Mark touched Mitch's arm.

"So? How was it?"

"What's to say? We did our duty. We sang for some folks, invited them to church. They shut their doors, went back to their lonely lives. You know how it goes."

"Did you hand out the packets?"

"We did."

"Good." Mark started down the hall, turning when Mitch called after him.

"You know, I'm still not sure what value all this had."

"Maybe you'll never be sure."

"So what's the point, then? None of them accepted our invitation to church tonight. They didn't care.

And the kids sure couldn't have gotten anything out of it. I just felt like—"

"You know something, Mitch? You go out there and serve God with this whiny, lazy attitude, and there's a good chance nothing *will* ever come of it, at least not the way you're going to see it. Maybe this is a test for you; I don't know. Sometimes you do the right thing because it's the right thing."

"Jeez, you sound like a pastor or something."

"Look, Mitch—"

"I got it; I got it. It's just . . . it's just tonight of all nights, you know?"

Pastor Mark's face softened, and he stepped closer.

Mitch continued. "I mean, when Rick was here, he mattered. He was interesting; he had good ideas; the kids thought he was exciting. Now, a year later, we've got 'em tooling around singing on porches— badly, I might add."

Mark put a hand on Mitch's shoulder. "I hear you, Mitch. I do. I want to talk to you about this when we have some time. Can we talk after the service?"

Mitch nodded. "I'm sorry. I'll let you go. Real quick, though: there was something tonight, kind of odd. Eva Boyle. Is she a little off? Something didn't seem right. I don't know what it was."

"Yeah, Eva Boyle. She's kept a lot of our ladies on their knees for some time. Her husband's been dead for years; he was terrible. Family's all scattered.

Some of them she hasn't seen in years, which I hear isn't necessarily a bad thing."

"Huh. You sure about that? She said they were all coming to see her tomorrow."

Pastor Mark squinted. "No, not likely."

"Well, that's great. Glad I followed through on my instincts."

Mark chuckled. "Maybe you could follow up with her sometime. I could go with you. Listen, Mitch, I know you didn't want to, but you did the right thing tonight. It was good for the kids, too. Thanks."

Eva

There was enough Sodium Pentothal and phenobarbital in her various prescriptions to kill a twelve-hundred-pound thoroughbred inside thirty seconds. The crystalline powder was odorless, so it would likely be tasteless, and the bouillon would take any edge off anyway. And then Eva would be gone. Painlessly. It would be frightening and quick, but she could do it.

She lifted the mug to her lips to test the temperature. Way too hot. She went to the freezer and dropped an ice cube into the mix. There, under a magnet on the refrigerator door, was a thirty-year-old picture of Eva with her kids in front of a Christmas tree. It had been there so long that it hadn't even registered with her for years. But now, on her last night, it stuck out. She pulled it off and studied it.

Lefty

Lefty finally turned onto Cornell Street and sucked in a deep breath. This was it. He passed half a dozen homes lit by thousands of Christmas lights and obnoxious lawn ornaments. Ironically, his childhood home stood out. No lights inside or out. He turned off his headlights and slowly pulled into the driveway, not wanting to attract attention.

He stared at the house. What was he doing? She was probably sleeping anyway.

Lefty sat waiting for a clear thought to muddle its way through his lubricated mind. Did he really need to hear "Merry Christmas" and say good-bye to his mother? He'd give it five minutes to make sure. If not, he only hoped his car would last another few miles so he could follow through on his original plan.

Eva

The drink had cooled. Eva was weary. She sat, her cup and picture on the dining room table, her hands in her lap, head down, shoulders slumped. The picture captured a moment so long ago that it was hard to even feel sad about it. She had been needed by her kids once, she wasn't anymore, and she was used to that.

Just take the drink. What are you waiting for?

The youth group's visit, along with the Christmas tree in the picture, made her think of church. How long had it been since she'd prayed?

"God," she whispered, "I'm sorry for anything I've done wrong by my family and for what I am about to do."

Was it too much to hope that God might accept her into heaven on Christmas Eve, even if she chose this heinous way of getting there?

Mitch

A picture of Mitch and Rick mountain climbing rested on Mitch's desk. Mitch remembered how confident he'd been about his future then. What was wrong with him now? He was still at the same church, still had a great group of kids, still enjoyed a supportive boss. If he couldn't thrive in this environment, he didn't deserve to. He would be frank with Pastor Mark after the service and try to assess the whole situation. Maybe Mark would agree it was time Mitch stepped down.

Mary

Mary wiped her face, stood, and paced to get some blood flowing. She briefly felt guilty for having left Jacob alone with the TV while she had a private moment. But she knew she'd needed it. Whenever she was anywhere with Jacob, he became something of a security blanket for her, even more than she was for him. She would hold him close, partly because she felt protective, but also because his presence tended to keep people from talking too openly about

Rick and what Mary was going through. That she hadn't needed him during her conversation with Kirk or her time alone on the sidewalk was something new.

She peeked through the window of her car to see the clock above the radio. It was getting late. She needed to get inside, deal with Jacob, and let Kirk finish the car. But that radio reminded her of her old routine on her drive to work. And for the first time in months, she prayed.

"God, I don't know what's going on. I'm angry at You, and I don't know where You are. I just needed to say that. That'll have to do for now."

Kirk

As he wandered the aisles, giving the poor woman some space, Kirk randomly straightened items. None was important. He sold little of real value.

What had his life become? He stopped and scanned his store. What could he do to get his life out of neutral? He had no idea.

Lefty

Five minutes had passed. Lefty still wanted to hear "Merry Christmas" and say good-bye.

FIFTEEN
10:20 P.M.

||||||||||||||||||||||||||||||||||||||||||||||||||||||||||||||||||||||||||||||||||||||||||||||||||||||||||||||||||||||||||||||||||||||||

Lefty

Lefty was struck by how little had changed at his childhood home. There were more cracks in the paint, but it was the same paint. And apparently, none of the times Animal Control had told his mom to fix the hole under the gutter had registered. Raccoons still had an obvious path into the attic.

He peeked through the dirt-speckled front window to see whether his mom was awake, or even home, and by the light from the streetlamp noticed the furniture hadn't moved in the years since he'd lived there. Maybe his mother was in her room in the back.

The old porch swing looked like it hadn't been used in a decade. As a kid, Lefty would sit there waiting for his father to come home from work. He could tell by the way his dad pulled into the driveway whether it would be a rough night. If the driving was erratic, Lefty would go inside immediately. If the car eased in and Dad emerged smiling, they would wrestle or toss a football.

Lefty lowered himself onto the swing. The chains were rusted and loud, and one of the boards was cracked. Finally satisfied it wouldn't collapse, he leaned back and closed his eyes, trying to relax, to think of good memories from this house. But his mind wasn't working well. He was exhausted and hungry, and he still had a booze buzz. He needed to make this quick.

He stood and moved to the door, drew in a long breath, and knocked. Nothing. He tried again.

Eva

Eva froze, her heart racing. Who could possibly be at the door at this hour? Surely no one up to any good. The first knock had jolted her from her thoughts, and now she feared for her safety. How ironic. She was planning to die tonight anyway, but the thought of someone else doing it terrified her.

She slowly stood and tiptoed to get a better angle on the door window. A man was peeking in. She stayed in the shadows as moonlight crossed his face. Eva gasped.

Luschel.

Lefty

Lefty was about to knock one last time when he saw his mother, wearing a nightgown with a green cardigan over it, shuffling toward the door. He took a step back and tried to appear casual—or at least not like a burglar.

Lefty's mother opened the door slightly. She looked so tired. It had been more than five years since he'd seen her, but she had aged much more than that. Of course, it didn't help that she looked upset.

"What are you doing here?"

"It's me."

"I know who it is."

"Why'd you have all the lights off? I saw you standing by the—"

"I didn't want to be bothered."

Why had he thought this would work? What did he expect, a prodigal son moment? Why would his mother, who had known him better than anyone, welcome him any more than anyone else would?

Eva

Eva couldn't decide whether to slap Luschel or hug him as tight as she was able. He looked awful—disheveled, eyes bloodshot. This was nothing new, but it was worse than normal. More than ever, he looked sad.

"Right. I'll just be going. . . ."

No, it couldn't end like this. That she might see one of her children tonight of all nights hadn't even crossed her mind. But now that Luschel was here, she needed to talk—to say good-bye in some way, even if it was awkward.

"So what are you doing here?"

"I just, well . . . I just came by . . . to get something, actually."

"Well, come on in. Let me take your jacket."

He didn't move. "Nah. I'm not staying. I'll leave it on." Luschel looked down and tapped the porch with his foot.

"How's Heather?"

"Ma, she ran out on me over two years ago."

"Now how would I know that?"

Luschel lifted his hands. "Okay, okay."

It wasn't like him to retreat like this. He looked so defeated.

"Life doesn't always turn out like we hoped," she said. "Does it?"

He shook his head and sighed. "You have no idea."

Her voice quavered. "Like heck I don't."

He wasn't making eye contact, and she feared he might bolt at any moment. She wouldn't be able to bear that. It would be too confusing, too incomplete.

"How are the kids? They okay?"

"Heather won't let me see them."

"Oh, now what have you done?"

"Ma . . ."

Why couldn't she just keep her mouth shut? She couldn't lay off him, even now?

"All right. So what do you want?"

"Nothing, I just—"

"Luschel, you scared me half to death." The other half was in her mug.

"Lefty, Ma. Lefty."

"Honestly, you're not even left-handed."

He slumped again.

She spoke softly. "Okay, Lefty. So you came to this house, on this night, for no reason?"

"Yeah, I got a reason."

"Well, what is it?"

He looked down again, shuffling. She forced herself to wait, willing to be silent for the first time.

"I came to say merry Christmas. Well, that ain't exactly right. I came here so you could wish *me* a merry Christmas."

"You need me to wish you merry Christmas?"

Lefty looked serious. He wasn't being sarcastic; he didn't look annoyed. He just stared.

"Why do you—?"

"Because you're my ma, that's all."

She was. Gazing at this beat-up, middle-aged man, she was immediately transported to the night he had come screaming from her womb, a precious child born into turmoil. Had he ever had a happy season, a time when family problems didn't cloud his eyes?

Was it possible this was really all he wanted? Something this simple? He *needed* something from her. When was the last time anyone . . . ?

143

"Well, I, uh . . . okay. Merry Christmas." She forced a smile, trying to look as sincere as she felt. But it hadn't come out right.

"Okay." He chuckled, obviously embarrassed, then turned away. "Look, I'm just gonna go—"

"No, please don't!"

He stopped.

"I'm sorry. It's just that this is so, um, unexpected. I mean—"

"Yeah, I know."

"Let me make you some tea or something. Are you hungry? I've got leftovers." There was an understatement.

"Ma . . ."

"No, hold on. I'll just be a minute. Come in."

Eva hurried to the kitchen before he could say no or see her lose control.

So many emotions flooded her. She walked into the kitchen with a purpose. She could wish her son a merry Christmas; she could serve her son a meal. She was his mom. And as long as she was alive, that would be true.

Eva emptied the killing pot into the sink.

Lefty

Lefty didn't want to stay much longer, but he was famished. If his mom was that eager to feed him, he would oblige.

She hurried about the kitchen, pulling food from

144

the fridge and plates from the cupboards. He didn't regret coming, but he had obviously flustered her. He didn't know if that was good or bad.

"I gotta admit," she said as she scurried about, "you're the best thing that's happened to me all evening."

"That right?" he said as he made his way past the dining room table and noticed a steaming mug. He picked it up on his way into the kitchen.

"You ever hear a group of teenagers sing 'Silent Night,' not a single note on key?"

"Not silent enough, huh?"

"Definitely not," she said, chuckling, but a look of alarm swept her face when she saw him lifting the mug to his mouth. "Luschel, no!" She rushed him and grabbed it, causing the hot liquid to spill onto his shoes.

"Ma, what are you—?"

"You didn't drink any of that, did you?"

"No. What is—?"

"I'm sorry. I have a cold and I didn't want you to get sick. I'm so sorry!" She handed him a towel, then went back to the food.

Maybe this was too much for her. He was obviously making her uncomfortable. But she would be hurt if he left now, right? He would stay. For her sake.

"Ma, you all right?"

"Me? I'm fine."

145

"Hey, it's Christmas Eve. Aren't you going to church?"

"Those carolers asked me that. Don't think I'll be able to make it this year."

"How come?"

"Well, I don't have a car anymore."

"What about the bus?"

"They changed the bus routes a year ago. Now the closest stop is all the way across the four-lane."

There was no one to take her to church? No friends, no one from the congregation? For as long as Lefty could remember, his mom had loved church, particularly the Christmas Eve service. Even his dad had attended that once in a while.

She pointed him to the small kitchen table as she put a plate of food in the microwave.

Kirk

Jacob continued to watch TV as Kirk stood behind the register, waiting for Mary. She paced outside with her back to the store, wiping her eyes. Kirk had four quarts of oil laid out in front of him and was ready to finish the job, but he wanted to give Mary her space.

She finally walked in, and her look suggested that nothing needed to be discussed.

"So tell me, Kirk, what were you going to do with your fortune?

"Don't know, actually. Never got that far. Doesn't really matter."

"Of course it matters. I, for one, am glad you didn't sell and move on, because I'd be stuck in the middle of nowhere trying to get a new Triple-A account."

"Well, that's true."

"See? It was all worth it."

They laughed, and Kirk raised his hands. "Absolutely. The last ten years all came down to my cleaning your air filter. This changes everything."

Mary

Kirk urged Mary to stay inside with Jacob while he finished her engine.

Mary crouched beside her son and put her arm on the back of his chair. Without a word, Jacob leaned in and rested his head on her shoulder. Tonight didn't feel so bad.

||||||||||||||||||||||||||||||||||||||||||||||||||||||||||||||||||||||||||||||||||||||||||||||||||||||||||||||||||||

Lefty

The food was good. It got extra points because Lefty hadn't eaten since scarfing down a few mini candy bars at the lawyers' office that morning. His fork and mouth didn't stop as he sat with his mom at the small kitchen table.

She needs something I can give. She loved to go to church, but she couldn't because she didn't have a ride. Well, he had a car.

"Your brother has no use for me anymore. I think he still blames me for your father."

"Kenneth's too good for all of us now. I wouldn't waste my time waiting on him."

"Heard from your sister?" she said.

"Nope."

"Me neither. Last I heard she was still *dancing.* I

149

used to get letters from her kids, but now I don't know what's going on."

"That right?"

"That girl's had a death wish since junior high. I don't know how she made it as far as she did."

"Well, it really wasn't all that far."

They fell silent again, and Lefty wondered whether he could leave a note telling the police to give her the car. Of course, then he would have to do the deed outside the car.

But what about tonight? She loved the Christmas Eve service. He could put off his plan for another hour or so and get her to and from church. A little Christmas Eve gift. Nothing big, but it was something.

Eva

From the way Luschel was eating, Eva knew the meal was a hit. Margaret's oddly timed visit hadn't been a waste after all, which made Eva feel less guilty about her lie to Dr. Lindell.

"I'm sorry about you and Heather, Luschel."

He shrugged. "I wasn't exactly man of the year."

"Don't lose touch with those kids, okay? It's no fun when your kids stop talking to you."

There it was. She had said it. She didn't want to spoil the evening, but she also needed to be on record.

"Okay, Ma, I get it."

"I'm just saying—"

"I get it."

"All right; I'm sorry." She was done with the nagging, she vowed. "Your cousin Jeffrey had another baby."

"How many is that now, two?"

"This makes four."

"Four. I don't know how he affords it."

"I don't know. But from what I hear, it's a beautiful baby."

"You know, Ma . . . I got a car."

"Okay . . ."

"If you needed to go to church tonight, I could take you."

Eva could barely breathe. Luschel had never offered to do anything for her. Why was he offering this now? There was so much to discuss, so much history, so many closeted skeletons. Would a simple ride to church make all of that unimportant? Did this offer make up for his having ignored her for so long?

For now, it sure felt like it.

"You'd do that for me?"

"If you needed me to."

Lefty

She *did* need him to. It was all over her face. She couldn't go to church, and he was her son, which made getting her there his responsibility. Wasn't that what children were supposed to do for their parents?

Children. I'm one of her children. A curious word for a middle-aged drunk about to do away with himself. *I am a child. Her child. Someone will miss me.*

She leaned forward. "Would you go in with me?"

"Oh, I don't think so."

"Oh, please, go in with me."

"I don't know, Ma. If I walk in there, the place might burst into flames."

Eva

They were going to church. Her son would take her.

She stood, wanting to hurry before he could change his mind. "I'm going to get dressed."

She took off her green cardigan, then put it back on over her red Christmas dress, the one she'd worn to every Christmas Eve service for ten years. She dabbed on a bit of makeup and touched up her hair. Then she pulled a pair of her late husband's dress shoes out of the closet.

She returned to the kitchen and held out the shoes. "Sorry about the spill, Luschel. Your father called these his—"

"Church shoes."

Eva worried Luschel might not want to wear anything of his father's, but he didn't hesitate to change into them. Nothing about his behavior tonight surprised her anymore.

She motioned to the containers of food on the counter. "Please take some of this with you."

"Nah. I don't really have room for it right now."

"But it's way too much for me. Please take some."

"Maybe we could just take it to the church," he said, looking uncomfortable.

"That's a good idea; I'm sure they'll know someone who could use it."

Luschel stood, then hesitated. "Ma, we got a problem. I don't have any money. If we're going to make it to church, we're going to need some gas."

"Oh." Wouldn't this be a cruel joke? They couldn't even afford to get to church until her nine dollars and fifty-two cents arrived from the bank. "I don't have any money either."

Wait! The carolers! She reached into her sweater pocket and pulled out the twenty, showing it to Lefty like a game show model.

Lefty

It wasn't the classiest thing in the world to offer someone a ride and then ask them to pay for it. But what else could he do? From the look on his mom's face, Lefty could tell she didn't mind.

Kirk

Everything Kirk could think to do for the car was done. This was the moment of truth. How humiliating would it be if, after all this time, he couldn't get it to work?

He wasn't a praying man, but as Kirk slid behind

the wheel and turned the key, "Please" escaped his lips.

The van roared to life as if nothing had ever been wrong.

Yes! Kirk pumped his fist. It was as satisfied as he'd felt in years.

Mary

Mary cocked her head. Was that the van? She saw Kirk lean in to the engine again; then he straightened and grinned at Mary, giving her a thumbs-up.

"Ready to go, Jacob?"

"Really?"

"The car's ready. Let me pay Kirk; then we'll say good-bye and go home, okay?"

Lefty

When Lefty got into his car, he quickly grabbed the gun from under his seat and stuffed it inside his pants before his mom opened the passenger door. He had to get rid of the gun. He had no idea what was happening in the near future or, for that matter, the very next day. But he knew one thing—he wasn't using a gun for a while. How could he?

This wasn't a big watershed moment or anything. He was still a loser, and in a few days he might have to reevaluate his future. But for now, he was tossing the gun. Tommy would have another, if necessary.

The gas gauge had flatlined. Lefty had no idea how the car had made it this far, but its time had come. As much as he didn't want to, he pulled back in to Mr. K's. His mom handed him the twenty.

Lefty walked to a trash can at the side of the gas station and grabbed a dirty paper bag from it. He emptied the bullets into his hand, slid the gun into the bag, and buried the bag in the trash, then tossed the bullets into the weeds.

Kirk

Mary had Jacob ready to go by the time Kirk came back in.

"I don't know how to thank you. How much do I owe you?"

"Mary, please."

"Kirk, you've got to let me give you something."

"Not another word. I'm serious."

Kirk heard the door and turned to see the same customer from before, the one who'd acted so bizarrely. He looked different—more sober, perhaps—but Kirk was wary.

"Hello there. Look, by law I can't give you that card back."

"Oh, that's okay. I got cash."

"All righty." Kirk moved to the register. A customer was a customer.

Mary

The guy looked less squirrelly somehow than the first time she'd seen him.

"You guys are back too, huh?" he said.

"Yeah. Car broke down."

"You been stuck here this whole time?"

"Yeah, but actually, Kirk here just fixed it. No charge."

"Fixed it free?" The guy looked at Kirk. "Wow. Not your typical gas station owner, huh?"

Mary gave Kirk a look, and he chuckled, reddening. If there was one thing she wanted him to know, it was that she knew he'd done a good thing. She imagined he didn't normally get much credit.

"Look," Kirk said, "if you're going to make it to your parents' . . ."

"My parents!" She looked at the guy. "We were going up to my parents' place for a late dinner, but now . . . excuse me; I have to call them."

Jacob pulled Mary's hand. "I'm hungry."

Lefty

"There's plenty of food in the freezer," Kirk said.

The woman waved him off. "No, it's fine. We need to get out of your way."

She got on the phone and walked down the aisle. Lefty saw her push her son's hand away from a candy bar he was reaching for. The kid was hungry. They obviously hadn't eaten a full meal. And as Lefty watched these two people who had unwittingly changed the course of his evening, he realized something: for the second time in one night, someone needed something Lefty could provide.

Lefty proudly handed Kirk the twenty. "Pump two. Sorry about before. Merry Christmas."

"Yep."

Eva

Eva found a portable CD player hardwired into the deck of Lefty's car. Perfect! She pulled the CD from her pocket and put it into the player, leaning back and closing her eyes as the music began.

Lefty

Lefty heard the music as he filled the tank. He recognized "It Came upon the Midnight Clear." He'd heard that song the last time he'd gone to a Christmas Eve service. He knew the song was about the angels on the night of Jesus' birth. But now he noticed it was about more than that.

> *And ye, beneath life's crushing load,*
> *whose forms are bending low,*
> *who toil along the climbing way*
> *with painful steps and slow,*
> *look now! for glad and golden hours*
> *come swiftly on the wing.*
> *O rest beside the weary road*
> *and hear the angels sing.*

Lefty hadn't heard angels singing much in his life. Even now, pumping gas outside a run-down convenience store in the middle of nowhere, he was homeless, jobless, and weary as they came. But while his mom waited in his car, he laid out containers of food for a stranded woman and her son, and the words of that song didn't seem so far-fetched.

SEVENTEEN

10:55 P.M.

||||||||||||||||||||||||||||||||||||||||||||||||||||||||||||||||||||||||||||||||||||||||||||||||||||||||||||||||||

Mary

"Mom, it's me again."

"Sweetie, are you close?"

"No, we're still here."

"Mary, what—?"

"Mom, we're fine. I'm sorry I didn't call earlier, but we've been busy working on the van. This guy at the gas station—he fixed the car, no charge."

"What do you mean? What guy? Are you okay? Were you and Jacob alone with a stranger?"

"Mom, please. We're fine. He was kind and helpful, and of course we were careful. He saved our behinds."

"So when are you coming?"

"I think we need to stay here. We can't drive tonight, obviously, and we need to be with Rick tomorrow."

"But—"

"Mom. We're spending the day at the home tomorrow. And I need you to understand that it would mean a lot to me if you and Dad came. And it would mean a lot to Jacob. Rick's always better when I'm around, so you don't have to worry about him acting out or anything."

Her voice quivered. "Mom, I know it's not easy, but I know he wants to see you. And I need you to do this for us because it's Christmas, and I want us all together, okay? Do you understand, Mom?"

"Honey, please don't cry. I'll talk to your father; we'll make it work."

"Tomorrow? You can come tomorrow?"

"Yes, we'll come tomorrow. Carl, we can leave tomorrow in the morning, right?! Yes, she's fine; she got help at the gas station! They're about to go home! She's going to stay there tomorrow, and we're going to go to them, okay?! Mary? Yes, we're coming tomorrow."

"Thank you, Mom."

"And you're okay? You're leaving now? Did you eat? What are you going to do for dinner?"

"We're fine. We'll grab some fruit or something at home before we go to bed. I'm going to get going, okay?"

"Okay, but you're sure you're all right? You'll be careful driving home, right? If the car acts up, just call the police if you can't reach anyone."

"I love you, Mom."

"And I love you, sweetie. Tell Jacob we love him and we'll see him tomorrow."

Kirk

Mary and Jacob approached the counter. She described her phone call and added, "Thank you so much. For everything."

"Sure," Kirk said. "And hey, thank you, too. It was good to—I don't know—breathe for a change, you know?"

"Yeah, I do. Hey, do me a favor, will you? Close the store. Go home. It's Christmas Eve."

"Will do." Kirk was so exhausted that he forgot it had been the slowest day of the year. "Let me walk you out. I've got to clean up anyway."

This was the awkward part. How do you say good-bye after such an odd night? Kirk knew he wouldn't likely see them again. That made sense. But parting now did seem sudden. What was he going to say? *Well, it was fun meeting you so we could open our souls to each other for a couple of hours. Best of luck with that whole brain-damaged husband thing, and don't forget to keep your car tuned up, ha ha.* Kirk wasn't any better at good-byes than he was at hellos.

He needn't have worried. As they stepped outside, Mary stopped, turned, and surprising Kirk, hugged him.

161

"Merry Christmas, Kirk."

"Merry Christmas, Mary."

Mary

When Mary had first walked into Mr. K's Quick Stop, she would have bet good money that she wouldn't end the evening hugging the man behind the counter. But this hadn't been a normal evening. By this point, she wasn't worried about Kirk taking her embrace the wrong way. They wouldn't likely see each other again. And when you say good-bye to a good friend you won't see again, you hug.

Another thing Mary would have bet against tonight was seeing a Christmas dinner stacked precariously on the shallow hood of her minivan. But this hadn't been a normal evening. She looked to Kirk for an explanation, but he was obviously as confused as she by the assortment of containers filled with turkey and vegetables. She pulled a penmanship-challenged note off the top and read aloud.

"'From my mom and me. It's really good. Lefty.'"

Mitch

The service was starting in two minutes. Mitch was not in the mood to hear the "reason for the season" or how "the most important Christmas gift was the One given two thousand years ago." Or for that matter, to sing the same carols he'd been singing all night. But the youth group kids were waiting for him in their usual spot near the front.

That was another of Rick's ideas that had become tradition. Teens had a reputation for being sullen and uninterested in church, but Mitch wanted this youth group to be different. So Rick suggested that instead of sitting in the back, where they could get away with messing around, they sit in front, forcing them to behave. He said this could make a subtle yet important statement that they cared, wanted to listen, and could be looked to as future leaders. At first the kids were annoyed and said they felt awkward, but after a lot of compliments from adults, they seemed to take pride in it.

So tonight, as always, Mitch would join them, whether he wanted to or not. If he could take them caroling, he could do this.

On the way past Pastor Mark's office, he glanced through the small window in the door. As always just before a service, Mark was on his knees next to his desk, eyes closed. Mitch headed into the sanctuary, knowing Mark was praying for more than just the sermon. He was probably praying for Mitch.

Eva

Eva hadn't seen Luschel smile all night until he got back into the car after dropping off the food. "Bet they won't expect that," he'd said.

They pulled into the church parking lot after

another ride devoid of conversation. Which was fine. Her son was taking her to church. At this point, Eva wasn't greedy. As they got out of the car, Luschel quickly pulled off his jacket and put on a bright red sweater he grabbed from the backseat. Eva chuckled. He was trying to dress up for church, but the loud sweater would only draw attention to his dirty pants and unkempt hair. No matter.

They stood next to the car, gazing at the huge, gorgeously lit building. Fearing Luschel might change his mind at any moment, Eva was careful not to rush him. He finally gave her a here-goes-nothing look, and they headed toward the entrance.

Amid the gauntlet of nods, smiles, and greetings, including a "So nice to have you back" from the usher holding the door, Eva made a decision. If Luschel thought this would be the last time he would take her to church, he was mistaken. She needed a good excuse to see him on a regular basis, and this was it. She was going to resume regular attendance at Grace Fellowship Church, and she would need a ride.

Mary

This was hardly a feast from a Dickens novel. The dinner involved a microwave, plastic forks, cans of soda, and the last package of paper plates for sale at Mr. K's. All were laid out with the food in front of three plastic folding chairs on the sidewalk, the whole bizarre picture illuminated by buzzing fluorescent lights.

Mary and Kirk had first discussed whether they dared eat food left by a stranger, but neither could imagine why someone would go through such an elaborate scheme just to poison random people. Past that, there was no way Mary was accepting the food for just her and Jacob. If Kirk didn't want her money, fine, but he could at least accept an invite to share an unexpected Christmas Eve dinner.

As they began to eat, Jacob whispered, "Mommy, is there cranberry sauce?"

"I don't think so, honey. That's your favorite, isn't it?"

Kirk jumped from his seat. "You, my man, are in luck. Wait one second."

Mary laughed. "Don't tell me you actually sell cranberry sauce in that place."

"Come on; it's a convenience store." He hustled inside.

Mary watched Jacob devour his food. "Doing okay, buddy?"

"Yeah. This is good. Tonight was fun."

Mary stared at her only child through misty eyes. Earlier that evening she had spontaneously issued a plea for help. At that moment her car broke down, and a few hours later here she was. Helped. In weird ways, yes. But helped nonetheless.

She still didn't understand why God allowed

certain things. She didn't know what He was doing with Rick or what He had in store for her and Jacob. But disaster prevention was never promised as a benefit of her faith. And perhaps that's what God was about—showing Himself faithful in a world thrown off course by humans with free will. God had given her Jacob, a greater gift than anyone deserved. And when she asked, albeit unknowingly, He'd given her the kindness and empathy of a gas station owner in the middle of nowhere. Maybe it was time to pay some attention. The least she could do was start going back to church.

Kirk

Jacob's face lit up as Kirk handed him a plate filled with cranberry sauce.

Mary shook her head. "I promise you, when he talks to his dad tomorrow, this will be the first thing he tells him about."

Kirk didn't tell her that it was the best thing anyone had said to him in a long time.

As they resumed eating in silence, Kirk glanced at the minivan. He had fixed it. He had been necessary. It hadn't been a mistake to be open on Christmas Eve. In fact, he would be open next year too.

Mitch

The sanctuary was filled with the usual preservice murmur of a packed house, accompanied by Christmas tunes from the organ. Zoned out, Mitch stared straight ahead, ignoring the jokes and laughter of the teens around him.

A nudge startled him out of his fog. Gretchen excitedly pointed toward the back. "Check it out; she came!"

"Who?"

"The old woman we met caroling. The last one, who acted funny. She came. See her with that guy? They're about to sit down. Maybe our visit helped, huh?"

Mitch barely recognized her with makeup and a pleasant look, but it was Eva Boyle. Of all the people they'd visited, she was the last one he thought would show. Was it possible their visit had stirred something in her? No way; the singing had been too bad.

Mitch watched her scan the room before meeting his eyes. She waved excitedly, grinning ear to ear. He waved back and gave a questioning look. She pointed at the middle-aged man next to her and mouthed, "My son."

Mitch smiled, and Eva lifted her hand to indicate the sanctuary, mouthing, "Thank you." Despite her radiant grin, he could see her eyes moisten from thirty feet away.

Thank you? Mitch had no idea what he or the kids had done. Maybe the note had moved her, or a song from the CD, or maybe she'd bribed her son to take her with the twenty bucks. It didn't matter. She was here, and she'd said thank you.

As Mitch slowly turned back around, he found himself thinking of Rick. He had been convinced that his visits made zero difference, that they were only awkward for him and meaningless for Rick. But he had also been convinced that tonight's caroling visits made zero difference, that there was no way anyone, let alone Eva Boyle, was coming to church because of them.

Well, here she was. So Mitch was going to see Rick tomorrow. Sometimes you do the right thing because it's the right thing.

Lefty

The lights dimmed, and the room quieted. Lefty stole a glance at his mother. She was glowing. As the orchestra started to play, her eyes widened and she sat up straighter. She turned to him, eyes welling.

"Isn't this wonderful?" she whispered.

He nodded.

"I'll need a ride on Sunday too, okay?" She turned back to the front before she could see him nod again.

This was his doing. Lefty's mother was beaming because of him. He might still be a no-account loser, homeless, unemployed, and with hardly a future. But someone needed him. He could get used to this.

Merry Christmas.

About the Authors

JERRY B. JENKINS (jerryjenkins.com) is the writer of the best-selling Left Behind series and author of over 170 books total. He owns the Jerry B. Jenkins Christian Writers Guild, an organization dedicated to mentoring aspiring authors. Former vice president for publishing for the Moody Bible Institute of Chicago, he also served many years as editor of *Moody* magazine and is now a member of the Institute's board of directors.

His writing has appeared in publications as varied as *Time*, *Reader's Digest*, *Parade*, *Guideposts*, in-flight magazines, and dozens of other periodicals. Jenkins's biographies include books with Billy Graham, Hank Aaron, Bill Gaither, Luis Palau, Walter Payton, Orel Hershiser, and Nolan Ryan, among many others. His books appear regularly on the *New York Times*, *USA Today*, *Wall Street Journal*, and *Publishers Weekly* best-seller lists.

Jerry is also the writer of the nationally syndicated sports-story comic strip *Gil Thorp*, distributed to newspapers across the United States by Tribune Media Services.

Jerry and his wife, Dianna, live in Colorado and have three grown sons and four grandchildren.

DALLAS JENKINS started Jenkins Entertainment with his father, Jerry B. Jenkins. Within a year, they developed, financed, and produced the $2 million independent film *Hometown Legend*. Dallas directed the short film based on this novel, *Midnight Clear*, starring Stephen Baldwin, which won a Crystal Heart Award from the Heartland Film

Festival and was the opening night selection at the San Diego Film Festival.

In 2006, Dallas was the co-executive producer of *Though None Go with Me*, a movie based on his father's book, which aired on the Hallmark Channel. His feature directing debut, also called *Midnight Clear*, recently won the Cinequest Film Festival award for Best First Feature. It will be released in December of 2007. Dallas has also written dozens of articles in nationally published magazines.

Dallas and his wife, Amanda, live in Los Angeles with their three children. He can be reached directly at dallas@ jenkins-entertainment.com.

An Interview with Actress Victoria Jackson

VICTORIA JACKSON was raised in a Bible-believing, piano-playing, gymnastic home with no TV. Her dad was a gym coach, so she competed in gymnastics from age five to age eighteen. She was also a cheerleader and a homecoming queen. Victoria attended Florida Bible College, received a gymnastic scholarship to Furman University, attended Auburn University for one year, and ended up in Hollywood, California, via summer stock in Alabama, where she met Johnny Crawford (of *The Rifleman* fame). Crawford put her in his night club act and later sent her a one-way ticket to the showbiz capital.

Victoria performed stand-up comedy for two years until *The Tonight Show* starring Johnny Carson put her act—which consisted of her doing a handstand while reciting poetry—on national TV. Following her twenty-two appearances with Johnny, she starred in several movies and TV shows, most notably *Saturday Night Live*.

In 1991 Victoria reunited with her high school sweetheart, married him, and moved to Florida, where he's a police helicopter pilot. As a mother of two, homemaking is Victoria's priority now, but she's always available to perform. Recently she has guest-starred on shows such as *The Naked Truth* and *The 700 Club*.

What is it like being a Christian in Hollywood?

I think being a Christian in Hollywood is the same as being a Christian in any other career. You are out-numbered and sometimes excluded or misunderstood. For example, my husband is on the police force, and he is a minority there just like I am when I go to work. In our workplaces, we both have to try to be a light in the darkness, be the ultimate professional for God's glory, and love our coworkers to the Lord.

When and how did you become a Christian?

I became a Christian at age six when I knelt by my bed next to my dad and asked Jesus to forgive me of my sins and come into my heart. Then I got baptized at our church, Carol City Baptist.

Did you feel pressure as the only Christian on *Saturday Night Live*?

At *Saturday Night Live*, I did not feel pressure being the only Christian. My dresser Beth Lincks was a Christian and prayed with me sometimes. Mary D'Angelo, my hair stylist, prayed with us too. Mostly, I focused on doing the best I could, not getting fired, and trying to keep up with the greatest comic geniuses of our generation!

One time I thought a sketch wasn't appropriate for me as a Christian to do, and I asked Lorne, the boss, if I could not be in it. He was very kind and understanding and gave the part to another actress. The dress rehearsal audience didn't laugh at the sketch, and it was cut from the show.

Have you always talked about your beliefs on set?

I have always tried to witness to my friends and coworkers throughout my life when it was appropriate of course.

What inspired you to become a part of this project? You are known for comedy. What made you take on a more serious role?

I was thrilled to be asked to be in my first Christian movie. I thought (director) Dallas Jenkins would do a great job. I'd met him once before. I thought the script was very good.

Which character do you most identify with?

I most identify with K Callan's character (Eva Boyle)—the lonely, older lady. Being forty-eight years old now, I keep wondering what my purpose will be when my kids leave the nest and the acting roles dry up. I know I'm supposed to serve God, but how? I like the verse in Psalm 92:14: "They shall still bear fruit in old age; they shall be fresh and flourishing." I hope I am still acting when I am an older woman. K did a great job and is beautiful.

Why is *Midnight Clear* an important story to both Christians and nonbelievers?

Midnight Clear is an important story because it is about hope. If we could see the big picture, like God does, we wouldn't give up on ourselves.

This movie deals with some serious issues. What would you say to people facing depression and suicidal despair?

What I would say to people facing depression and despair is (a) they are not alone—many of us have felt the exact same way, (b) we all have failures and sadness in our lives, (c) read the Bible and pray, (d) with faith the size of a mustard seed you can see the sun again and be useful and happy, (e) pray "God, I believe; help Thou mine unbelief" and He will, (f) and think about someone else. Helping others always brings a high!

OFFICIAL SELECTION
CINEQUEST
FILM FESTIVAL

MIDNIGHT CLEAR

STEPHEN BALDWIN

One night.

Five strangers.

Hope comes in unexpected places.

BASED ON THE SHORT STORY BY BEST-SELLING AUTHOR JERRY B. JENKINS

JENKINS ENTERTAINMENT PRESENTS A DALLAS JENKINS FILM "MIDNIGHT CLEAR"
STEPHEN BALDWIN KIRK B.R. WOLLER MARY THORNTON MITCHELL JARVIS RICHARD FANCY VICTORIA JACKSON AND K CALLAN
CASTING BY BEVERLY HOLLOWAY MUSIC BY JEEHUN HWANG COSTUME DESIGNER STEPHEN CHUDEJ EDITOR FRANK REYNOLDS PRODUCTION DESIGNER JAMES CUNNINGHAM
DIRECTOR OF PHOTOGRAPHY RANDALL WALKER GREGG EXECUTIVE PRODUCER JERRY B. JENKINS PRODUCERS KEVIN DOWNES DALLAS JENKINS WRITTEN BY WES HALULA DIRECTED BY DALLAS JENKINS

JENKINS
ENTERTAINMENT

For details and a preview of *Midnight Clear* and
other films by Jenkins Entertainment, please visit
www.jenkins-entertainment.com.

CP0183

From *New York Times* best-selling author
Jerry B. Jenkins

A condemned man with nothing to lose

meets one with nothing to gain,

and everyone washed

by the endless ripples

of that encounter

recalls the day

a bit of heaven

invaded

a lot of hell.

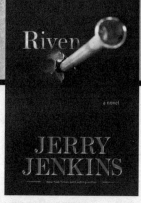